Favourite Fairy Tales From Grimm

Favourite Fairy Tales From Grimm

Retold by Jane Carruth
Illustrated by Benvenuti

HAMLYN

London · New York · Sydney · Toronto

HERE ARE THE STORIES IN THIS BOOK:

Published 1972 by The Hamlyn Publishing Group Limited
London · New York · Sydney · Toronto
Hamlyn House, Feltham, Middlesex, England
© Copyright this edition, The Hamlyn Publishing Group Limited 1972
© Copyright 1970 by Editions des Deux Coqs d'Or, Paris
and Mondadori — OGAM, Verone.
Printed in Czechoslovakia by Svoboda

ISBN 0 600 31712 9
51099

Jorinda and Joringel

In an old castle in the middle of a dense forest lived an evil witch. In the day-time she changed herself into a sleek black cat or a huge owl. But at night she took her proper witch-woman shape.

Now, if any travellers came within a few hundred yards of the castle, the witch had the power to enslave them for ever.

Many a pretty young girl from the nearby town was captured in this way and changed into a bird. The witch kept her birds in big wicker cages inside the old castle.

One lovely summer's day, two young people whose names were Jorinda and Joringel came to the forest. They were lovers and they walked hand in hand, talking in low voices about the day they would be married.

They were so much in love that they lost all count of time and of where their footsteps were taking them. Alas, when it was too late, the young man realized that they were only a short distance from the witch's castle.

Before he had time to drag Jorinda away, he saw her change into a nightingale, whilst in the tree above his head a large screech owl stared down at him with burning eyes.

Then the owl began flying round and round the poor little bewildered nightingale, driving her towards the castle with loud to-whoos.

When Joringel tried to give chase, he found that his feet were rooted to the ground.

Just as the sun was setting the screech-owl returned, flew once round the young man's head and then disappeared into the thicket.

Presently, an old woman appeared. Her skin was as yellow as ancient parchment and she had a nose as crooked as a butcher's meat hook.

As she stared up at him, Joringel found that he could move once again and he fell down on his knees in front of her.

'Give me back my beloved Jorinda,' he begged, tears filling his eyes. 'She is all I have in this world.'

'You will never see her again,' said the old witch, with a cackle. 'Seven thousand maids sing and twitter in my wicker-basket cages. She is but one more captive.'

And with that she went away towards her castle. When Joringel heard the door slam and the rattle of the bolts, he made up his mind to stay as near to the castle as he dared.

But he had no money, so in order to live he obtained employment as a shepherd in one of the villages on the far side of the forest.

At night, when his work of guarding sheep was done, he went back to the forest.

Some nights he even slept in the forest to be closer to his beloved Jorinda and, on one such night, he had a dream.

He dreamt that he came upon a flower, blood-red in colour, which held a wondrous pearl. In his dream, Joringel plucked the flower. Then, holding the flower, he went to the castle. No sooner did he touch the castle door with this flower than it swung open and, once inside the castle, everything he touched with the flower was instantly freed from enchantment.

Joringel remembered his dream so vividly that he decided to search for the flower.

For many days he searched in vain. Then on the ninth day he came upon a flower which was blood-red in colour and which held a dew-drop as big as a fine pearl.

Joringel plucked the flower and holding it carefully set out on his long journey back to the castle.

When at last he reached the witch's stronghold, he touched the big, heavy door with his magic flower and it swung open.

'The flower is just like the flower in my dream,' Joringel thought. 'Now I must find the place where that wicked witch keeps all the birds.'

But the castle was a maze of narrow passages and Joringel went down one and then a second without finding what he sought.

At last, he stood still and suddenly the deep silence was broken by the sweet song of the nightingale.

Now Joringel had only to follow the sound until he came to a vast room. Here, from ceiling to floor were thousands of wicker cages all filled with birds.

And there, before one of the cages, was the witch herself, pushing bread through the bars.

When she saw him, the witch spat at him and tried to come close, but Joringel held up the magic flower which kept her at a distance. The witch's red eyes filled with hate as she backed away.

Joringel was certain now that his magic flower was proof against her evil spells but he still had to find his Jorinda.

He stared in dismay at the hundreds upon hundreds of nightingales in their cages.

'How can I ever decide which of these birds is Jorinda?' he asked himself.

As he stood there, he caught a glimpse of the witch stealing from the room with one of the cages in her hand.

Quick as a flash, Joringel turned about and sprang towards her, wresting the cage from her claw-like hands.

The brown nightingale fluttered towards the bars as Joringel stretched out his precious flower. At a single touch of its magic petals, the bird changed into a lovely young girl — Jorinda!

Joringel held her in his arms for a moment, then he advanced upon the wicked witch, crushing his flower against her cloak before she could escape him. As she screeched her loud defiance, she changed into a lizard and vanished from sight.

With the witch out of the way, Joringel was free to go round the thousands of cages with his magic flower and bird after bird became happy, laughing maidens once again.

'We shall never forget you,' they promised brave Joringel, as they set out for their homes.

'And we shall never forget you,' Joringel told them, as he took Jorinda's hand in his. 'You are welcome to come to our wedding'

Then, with a backward glance at the old castle, the ruins of which you might easily come across if you could find the forest, the happy pair set out for home.

The Four Musicians

There was once a poor old donkey who served his master well for many years. Then one day his master said to him. 'You don't seem to be working as well as you used to, so I am going to give you a sound beating just to make you work a little harder.'

This was too much for the donkey and he made up his mind to run away that same day.

Now in the same part of the country there was an old hunting dog who had served his master well for many years. Then one day his master said to him, 'You can't run as fast as you used to. In fact you are not worth your keep so I am going to have you destroyed in the morning.'

This was too much for the dog and he made

up his mind to run away that very same day.

Donkey and Dog met up with each other on the road that led to the big city.

'What are you doing so far away from home?' demanded Donkey when he saw the dog.

'Alas,' replied Dog. 'When I grew too old to chase rabbits for my master he said he was going to have me killed. So I ran away.'

'Much the same sort of thing happened to me,' said Donkey. 'Let's make for the city and become musicians. I am very musical, you know.' And he brayed loudly.

'So am I,' said Dog, and he barked loudly.

The two new friends had only gone a little way down the road when they came upon a most miserable looking cat. Her fur was all wet and she looked as if she could scarcely put one paw in front of another.

'Whatever is the matter with you?' asked Donkey.

'Alas,' said the cat, 'my mistress tried to drown me in a pail of water just because I didn't catch as many mice for her as I did yesterday.'

'Then you had better join us,' said Dog. 'We are two musicians on our way to the big city to form a band.'

'I shall be delighted, I'm sure,' purred Cat, 'I sing very well.'

The three friends were still many miles from the big city when they came upon rather

a grand looking cock sitting on a fence all by himself. 'Hi!' called out the cock. 'Where are you three going?'

'We're off to form a band in the big city,' Donkey told him. 'With a voice like yours you ought to be in our band, too.'

'Nothing I would like better,' crowed the cock, 'for I happen to be looking for a change of residence.'

'You mean you're running away, I suppose,' said Dog. 'Well, come with us.'

So Cock joined the three friends and all four went down the road together, with Cock riding on Donkey's back. And on the way he told them his own sad story.

'There's not much to it,' said Cock, 'I just

happened to overhear my mistress tell my master that she meant to boil me for her Sunday dinner, that's all!' And he shook out his tail feathers.

Cat purred in deep sympathy, Dog howled and Donkey brayed and all three comforted the cock and made him crow loudly.

So the four friends went along until they reached a deep, dark forest.

'It's growing dark,' said Cock, 'if I may, I would like to suggest we find a place in the forest where we can be comfortable for the night.'

Dog, Cat and Donkey all agreed that this was a splendid idea, and so the four friends entered the forest.

Presently, Donkey made a suggestion. 'As it is growing very dark,' he said, 'I think Cat should go ahead and spy out the land.'

'Excellent idea!' purred Cat, who was proud of her keen eyesight. 'I'll do that!'

Off she went, but was soon back, her fur on end with excitement. 'You'll never guess,' she began, 'but beyond these trees there's a house with a light in the window!'

'Sleeping in a house will be much better than sleeping in the forest,' said Dog.

'Not so fast,' said Donkey. 'We must make sure the house is empty. I tell you what, we

15

can all peep inside that window if Dog can stand on my head and Cat on Dog's back and Cock on top of Cat.'

This was hailed as a very good idea, and soon all four friends were looking through the lighted window. And what do you think they saw?

Four fierce looking men, who were really desperate robbers, sat round a table eating and drinking.

The robbers were much too drunk to believe their eyes when they saw the animals at the window. And soon they went back to their feasting.

Meanwhile, Donkey was consulting with his friends how best they could get into the house.

'I don't like it,' said Cat nervously. 'These men looked so fierce that it is very likely they would kill us if they could.'

'But we mustn't give them the chance,' said Donkey. 'We must drive them away,' he went on solemnly. 'And this is how we'll do it.'

When his friends understood his plan they all prepared themselves to burst through the window just as the robbers were drinking the last drop of their ale.

With a great crash and a splintering of glass, Donkey broke the window with a flash of his hooves.

Then came the moment of attack. Braying loudly, Donkey kicked out wildly at the nearest robber.

Crowing shrilly, Cock pecked at the head of another robber.

Miaowing loudly, Cat scratched the hands of yet another robber, and growling fiercely Dog bit the legs of the last robber.

There was so much noise and confusion that the robbers thought they were being attacked by evil spirits and fled into the forest.

Then, feeling very pleased with themselves, the four musicians sat down at table and began to eat the food the robbers had left.

'Our plan worked,' said Donkey proudly. 'We can eat and drink to our fill and then settle down for a quiet night's rest.'

'I'll keep watch,' said Cat, as Donkey blew out the light.

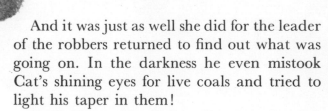

And it was just as well she did for the leader of the robbers returned to find out what was going on. In the darkness he even mistook Cat's shining eyes for live coals and tried to light his taper in them!

Scratching and spitting, Cat flew into his face — and that was the very end of the robbers, for when their leader returned he told them that the evil spirits were far too powerful to be driven away.

By morning, the four musicians liked the house so well that they made up their minds to stay and to begin practising at once.

So if, by chance, you are in that forest and you hear the sound of music you can be certain that it is the four musicians hard at work!

17

The Seven Ravens

Once upon a time there was a man who had seven sons. But though he loved his sons he still longed with all his heart for a little daughter. And at last his wish was granted. His wife bore him a lovely baby girl.

But the baby when she was born was so tiny and frail that her father cried out in alarm, 'We must have her baptised at once.'

Then he turned to his eldest boy and said, 'Take this jug and run down to the well with it and fill it with water.'

'We'll all go!' shouted the youngest son. And all seven boys rushed off to the well.

But the boys were so eager to fill the jug that they began to jostle each other as soon as they reached the well.

'Let me be the one to fill the jug for our new baby sister's baptism,' cried one.

'No, no, let me!' cried another. And a third cried, 'We should all have a turn!'

You can guess what happened next. There was so much pushing and shoving, so much argument, that the jug fell to the ground and was broken.

The seven brothers looked at each other in dismay, the broken jug at their feet.

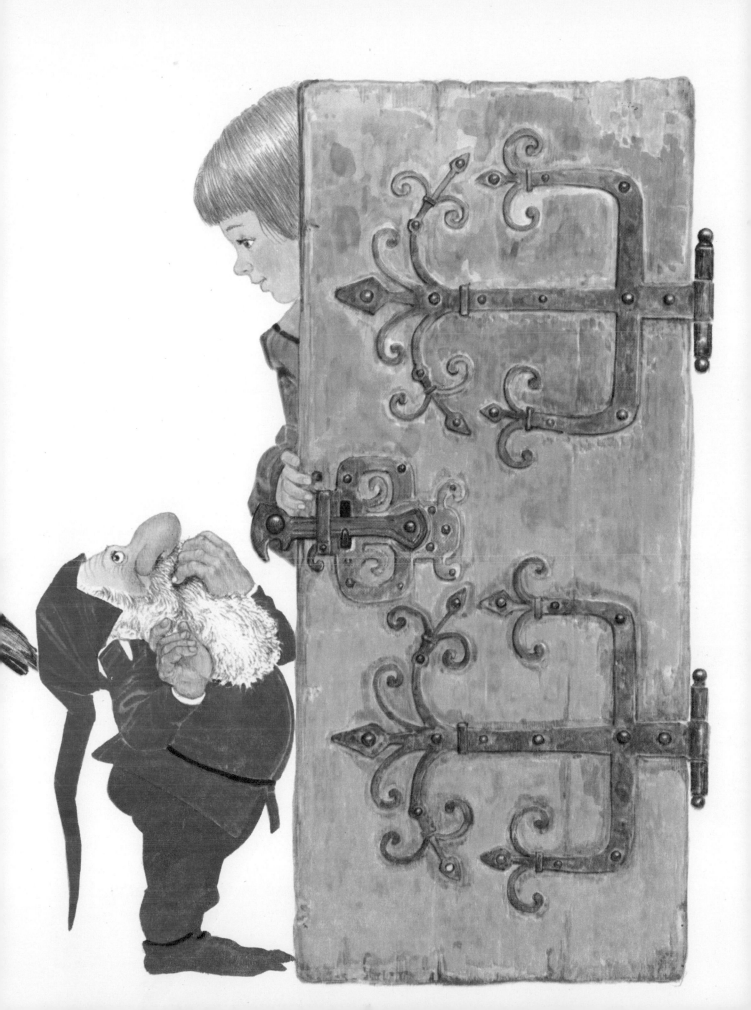

'What shall we do?' they asked each other. 'We dare not go back and tell our father. He will be angry at the way we have behaved.'

Meanwhile, their father waited impatiently for their return and when they did not come, he cried out in sudden anger, 'I wish my sons were turned into ravens!'

Scarcely were the words out of his mouth when he heard the sound of beating wings above his head. He looked up into the sky and saw seven ravens, black as night, flying away.

No words of mine can tell you of the horror and fright that filled that father's heart as he saw them go.

The father had lost his sons but he had gained a daughter for in spite of being so tiny and frail the child lived.

And she grew into a lovely young girl — so kind and gentle to everyone that she was greatly loved.

Then one unhappy day Gretel, for that was her name, was walking in the garden when she heard two neighbours talking.

A thick hedge screened Gretel from their eyes and so they talked loudly and freely not knowing that she was there.

'Such a nice child,' said one, 'and so pretty.'

'Yes,' said the other, 'Gretel is the apple of her father's eye, but sometimes I think he looks sad that he has lost his seven sons.'

'Of course he is sad,' said the other woman. 'And to think it was all through Gretel that he lost them . . .'

Gretel waited to hear no more but rushed indoors to her father to ask him what these strange words meant.

Her father grew pale when she began talking about her seven brothers for he had hidden the truth from her. But Gretel would not leave him until, at last, her father told her the whole sad story.

'I spoke the words in a rage,' he said gently, 'little knowing what the result would be. Do not fret, pretty one, it is not your fault that your brothers are now seven coal-black ravens flying betwixt the sun and the moon.'

When Gretel heard the full story, she wept and ran to her room and from that day she knew no peace. At last she determined to set out in search of her seven lost brothers. 'I will take only a few things with me,' she told herself. And she selected a little ring which her mother had given her, a loaf of bread and a pitcher of water. Last of all she picked up a small chair so that she might sit on it when her legs grew too tired to carry her.

Then she set out. 'I will travel the whole world,' she told herself. 'First, I will journey to the sun. The sun is so big and strong and he sees so much. He will know where my brothers are!'

So little Gretel journeyed to the sun.

And some of the way was cold and hard and much of the way was blisteringly hot. When at last she reached the sun, he was so burned up and disagreeable that she dared not stay long enough to tell him her story for fear he would burn her up too!

'Perhaps the moon will be kinder to me,' Gretel thought, as she ran away.

But the moon was no kinder. The lady moon was cold and hard and talked only of herself and Gretel saw that she would never get an answer from her.

Then she hurried to the stars. And the stars wery sorry for Gretel. They told her to sit down on her little chair and listen. Then the shiniest of all the stars said, 'We know where your brothers are. They are inside the glass mountain.'

'Then I shall go to the glass mountain and let them out,' Gretel cried happily.

'Not so fast,' said the morning star, who was the kindest, 'you cannot get through the door into the glass mountain without this.' And he handed Gretel the drumstick of a chicken.

Gretel accepted the drumstick gratefully, wrapped it in her handkerchief and set off for the glass mountain. But, alas, by the time she reached the glass mountain she had lost the magic drumstick which would unlock the door.

Gretel was almost in tears until she thought her little finger perhaps might do instead. It hurt a lot to use her finger as a key, but the door swung open.

Once inside, she was met by a tiny dwarf who asked her what she wanted.

'I am looking for my brothers,' she told him. 'They are seven ravens.'

'Come into the room,' the dwarf invited her, stepping to one side. 'They will soon be returning for it is their mealtime.'

Gretel watched as the dwarf fetched the ravens' dinner. He set down the food on seven little plates and then he fetched seven little glasses of water. Gretel took a morsel from each of the seven plates and a sip of water from each of the seven glasses. But in the last little glass she dropped the ring.

Then the dwarf returned and, as he did so, Gretel heard the whirring of birds' wings.

'My Lord Ravens are returning,' the dwarf said. And Gretel hid herself, overcome with fear, behind the door.

When the ravens saw that someone had been at their food and drink, they croaked their astonishment. Then the seventh and youngest of the ravens found the ring in his glass and croaked, 'Look what is in my glass! Our mother's gold ring. I know it well!'

Then the oldest raven croaked, 'Only our sister could have brought this ring. Pray God she is here — for her presence in the glass mountain will break this evil spell.'

When Gretel heard these words, she rushed out and the ravens instantly took on their proper shapes.

Then the seven brothers hugged and kissed their brave little sister and joyfully set out for home.

Hansel and Gretel

There was once a woodcutter who had two children, a boy and a girl, called Hansel and Gretel.

When his wife died, the woodcutter married again and it soon became clear that his new wife would never love his two children as he did. To make matters worse, a famine fell upon the land, and the woodcutter found it more and more difficult to make a living.

Soon, all his savings were gone and there was very little food left.

One night, whilst the children slept, his wife said to him, 'What are we going to do, husband? All our savings are gone.'

The woodcutter groaned and buried his face in his hands. 'Day after day, I ask myself that very same question,' he said at last.

'Then I'll give you an answer,' returned his wife, and she lowered her voice. 'We must get rid of the children.'

Her husband was so startled at this that he raised his head. 'What are you saying?' he exclaimed. 'What do you mean?'

Forgetting to keep her voice lowered, the woman shouted, 'I'll tell you what I mean. We must rise early in the morning and take the children deep into the forest where we shall leave them.'

'How can you suggest such a cruel deed?' cried the woodcutter. 'If we leave the two children in the forest we shall very likely never see them again.'

'And then there will be two less mouths to feed,' retorted his wife. 'I tell you, husband, we shall die of starvation unless we do something soon.'

As the pair argued this way and that, the sound of their voices roused Hansel from his sleep and he crept to the top of the stairs to listen.

'Very well,' he heard his father say, at last, 'you will have your way. We'll take the children into the forest in the morning and leave them there.'

Hansel crept back to bed and told Gretel what he had heard. 'Don't worry,' he said. 'I've thought of a plan already.'

As soon as the cottage was silent, Hansel got up, pulled his jacket over his pyjamas and crept downstairs.

The back-door was unlocked and soon Hansel was in the garden filling his pockets with smooth round pebbles.

'When we set out tomorrow,' he told his sister, as soon as he was safely upstairs, 'I mean to leave a trail of pebbles behind us as we go along. These pebbles will lead us safely back home.'

Early the next morning, Hansel was wakened by his stepmother's loud voice.

'Get up this minute!' he heard her shout.

And he called back, 'We're coming!' Then he went to Gretel and shook her gently.

'Hurry, little sister,' he said. 'And be brave. Remember — don't say a word about the pebbles.'

Their stepmother thrust two slices of dry bread into their hands when they came downstairs. 'We are going into the forest,' she told them, 'to get some wood. It will be a long day so don't eat the bread now but save it for later.'

As they set out, their father gave them a long sad look, and Hansel knew that he was thinking of the moment when he would leave them all alone in the forest.

Hansel gave his father a brave smile for the pebbles that made his pockets so heavy were very comforting and he was not afraid.

They set out in single file, his father leading, then came his stepmother, then his sister. Hansel, himself, came last and this was how he planned it.

As he lingered behind, he dropped his shiny pebbles, one by one.

'Why do you drag your feet so?' his stepmother asked sharply, as she looked back at him over her shoulder.

'I am watching the sun rise over the rooftops,' Hansel replied.

As they went on, farther and farther into the forest, the trees were so tall and thick that their branches blotted out the sun.

'We shall stop here,' their stepmother said at last, and the woodcutter said, 'You must help me to build a fire.'

Hansel and Gretel ran this way and that in their efforts to collect sticks. Soon they were so tired that they were glad to sit down and watch their father light the fire.

'You can rest here and eat your bread,' said their stepmother. 'Your father and I will go farther into the forest and come back for you when the sun begins to set.'

In spite of what he knew, Hansel almost believed his stepmother.

'Don't worry about us,' he said. 'We shall stay by the fire until you return.'

But the children were so weary after their long walk that very soon they fell asleep.

When they awoke, the fire had burned out and the forest was dark.

Gretel opened her eyes wide and shivered.

'What shall we do, Hansel?' she asked, in a voice that shook with fear. 'They have left us all alone. We shall never find our way home.'

'Oh yes, we will,' said Hansel. 'If we wait a little while longer the moon will rise and we shall be able to see the pebbles.'

Gretel stopped shivering and Hansel put an arm round her shoulders as they waited.

Presently, the moon began to rise in the sky and soon the forest was bathed in a silvery light.

'Now we can see the pebbles!' Hansel cried joyfully and, taking his sister by the hand, he soon found the last of the pebbles he had dropped.

'We are on the trail,' he told Gretel. 'All we have to do is follow it.'

The children walked for most of the night.

'There's not much farther to go,' said Hansel as he saw the smoke from the cottage chimney spiralling above the trees. 'Come on, Gretel, let's run the last part of the way.'

Their stepmother opened the door in answer to Hansel's knock and almost at once she began to scold them, pretending it was their fault, not hers, that they had got left behind in the forest. But their father, when he saw them, was overcome with joy and hugged them as if he would never let them go.

Soon after this, the poor woodcutter found himself telling his wife that they were just as badly off as before.

'Then we must do something about it,' said

his wife and, just as before, she lowered her voice for the children had not long since gone upstairs to bed. 'We must take them even farther into the forest this time.'

'No, no, I cannot bring myself to do such a thing twice over,' protested the woodcutter.

And for answer, his wife went to the cupboard and fetched a loaf of stale bread.

'Look, husband,' she cried bitterly, and she held up the miserable piece of bread so that the woodcutter was forced to look at it. 'This is all we have between us and starvation. I tell you we must do this thing.'

'Very well, wife,' replied the poor man, and he sighed heavily. 'In the morning we shall take the children into the forest and leave them there.'

Now, by good fortune, Hansel had kept awake and hearing the raised voices, he crept to the top of the stairs and listened.

'I will fill my pockets with pebbles as I did before,' he told himself, when he heard his father at last agree to his wife's plan.

But, this time, when Hansel reached the backdoor that led into the garden, to his horror, he found it locked and the key gone.

In the morning, the woodcutter led the way into the forest as before, and Hansel dropped crumbs of bread, thinking they would serve as well as the pebbles.

His stepmother scolded him for being so slow. But Hansel told her, 'I am trying to catch a glimpse of the big fat pigeon on our roof-top.'

The woodcutter took his family even farther into the forest and the children were glad to sit down and watch him build a fire.

'We shall leave you here by the fire,' the woodcutter told Hansel and Gretel. 'But we shall come back for you later in the day.'

The fire's dancing flames soothed the two children and soon Gretel put her head on Hansel's shoulder and fell fast asleep.

Hansel slept, too, and when he awoke it was already dark.

'In a moment the moon will rise and show us the trail of breadcrumbs,' he told his sister, as he shook her gently awake.

Gretel rubbed her eyes and looked as if she were going to burst into tears, but her brother pulled her to her feet.

'Don't be afraid,' he said. 'We'll soon be safely home.'

But, oh, how wrong he was, for when the kindly moon shed her silver light on the grass there were no breadcrumbs to be seen. The birds of the forest had eaten them all up.

'It can't be helped,' Hansel said bravely. 'We shall just have to find our own way.'

All through the long night and part of the next day, the children walked. Gretel was so tired and hungry that she begged her brother to rest.

'No, no, Gretel, we must try to find the path that will lead us out of the forest,' he told her.

When night fell on the first day, they found a sheltering bush and curled up behind it. And in the morning, Hansel found some berries which he knew were safe to eat and shared them with Gretel.

They walked fewer miles on the second day and on the third day, Hansel was so weary himself that he could no longer even pretend to be cheerful.

He was almost ready to give up when all at once he saw a beautiful white bird perched on the branch of a tree.

'Look, Gretel!' he whispered. 'That white bird, it seems to be wanting us to follow it.

27

See how it flies a little way and then stops and looks back!'

Hand in hand, the two children ran after the white bird, their tiredness forgotten, until presently they saw before them the strangest house they had ever seen in their lives.

The roof was made out of bread and the walls were covered with cakes. Sugar sticks served as window-frames, and the steps were fashioned out of hard brown toffee.

'I am so hungry I could eat a — a house!' Hansel laughed, and he ran forward and broke off a piece of gingerbread roof.

'And I could eat all the cakes in the world,' cried Gretel, and she laughed and ran forward and broke off a piece of cake wall.

As the two children ate the bread and cakes and sugar sticks, the door of the wonderful house suddenly opened and an old, old woman appeared on the step.

Hansel gulped and began to feel afraid but the old woman gave him a crooked smile.

'Do not be afraid of me, my little man,' she croaked. 'And do not hide behind your brother, my sweet little maid,' she said, turning her red eyes on Gretel, who was even more afraid than Hansel.

'We didn't mean any harm,' said Hansel.

'Of course not, my lovelies,' said the old

woman. 'Come inside and I will see to it that you have all the food you can eat.'

The children lost their fear completely as the old woman sat them down at a table laden with good things to eat.

There were apples and pears and big sugar plums, nuts and sweets and cakes filled with jam and cream.

'Eat all you can,' said the old woman, 'and when you have finished I will show you where you can sleep.'

Hansel and Gretel forgot everything but the joy of feeling safe again, and when their new friend showed them the two pretty pink beds, they were delighted.

Now, as you may have already guessed, that old woman was a witch. Witches have red eyes and voices that cackle and croak. Some even have long hooked noses and walk with stout crutches.

This witch had all these things and besides, a most terribly cruel nature. Whenever she was hungry, she would send out her snow-white bird into the forest to lure children to her cottage. Once the children were in her power, she kept them prisoner until they were fat enough to eat.

Early the next morning, she grabbed hold of Hansel and pulled him out of bed.

'Into the cage you go,' she cackled, 'until you are fat enough to eat.'

Hansel was taken so completely by surprise that he did not even struggle, but Gretel let out a loud sob when she saw what was happening to her brother.

'As for you,' croaked the witch, turning on Gretel. 'You will be my servant until I have eaten your brother. Then I will eat you too. Now, be off with you to the well and fetch me some water.'

'I must be brave,' Gretel told herself, as she ran down to the well. 'I must find a way to help Hansel.'

When she returned, the witch made her scrub the kitchen floor and tidy up the cottage.

'You won't starve, I promise you,' said the witch, when this was done. 'You'll have to make do with scraps until your turn comes. But your brother will have the best.'

True to her witchy word, the old woman fed Hansel on chicken and cream and dumplings and strawberry jam. But the witch, after the manner of all witches, had very poor eyesight so she could not tell if Hansel was growing fat. Instead, she would ask him to put his finger through the bars so that she could feel it.

Hansel, however, had found a way to trick her. In his cage was an old chicken bone and he put this through the bars for the witch to feel.

'How is it that you stay so thin and bony?' she cried on the tenth day. 'I will not wait. I have made up my mind to eat you tomorrow, thin or fat.'

Early the next morning, the witch said to Gretel, 'Be he thin or fat I am going to eat your brother today. Now fetch me water from the well, and set out the flour and the mixing bowl.'

Gretel did as she was told though she could scarcely see for the tears that kept coming into her eyes.

At first, she thought the witch was going to make a huge pie and put Hansel in it but then it became clear that the witch was going to bake some bread first before roasting Hansel.

She watched the witch light the huge oven and, when the heat from it was beginning to spread into the kitchen, she asked the witch in a trembling voice what she was going to do first.

'A sensible question,' said the witch, who was in a very good mood, 'I'm going to bake the bread first and I'll be obliged if you'll put your head inside the oven and tell me how hot it feels.'

'She's going to bake me with the bread,' Gretel suddenly thought. 'I'm sure she is!'

So she pretended to fumble with the oven door and when the witch told her to be quick

about it, she whispered, 'The door is much too heavy for me to open.'

Impatient to get on with her plans, the old witch hobbled over to the big oven door and wrenched it open.

Quick as a flash, Gretel sprang forward. With all her strength she pushed the witch so that she fell into her own oven. Then the brave little girl slammed shut the door.

With the speed of a deer, Gretel ran to the cage which held her brother.

'Hansel! Hansel!' she cried. 'The witch is roasting inside her own oven. I can let you out. We are saved!' And she opened the cage door and set Hansel free.

How they hugged and kissed each other, and when Hansel heard what his sister had done, he laughed aloud.

'Let's take what we can,' he said. 'Let's search her house for treasure before we set out for home.'

And what treasures they found — two chests stuffed with diamonds and rubies and pearls!

'We have a right to take as much of this as we can carry,' declared Hansel, beginning to fill his pockets, 'for a witch's treasure belongs to anyone who finds it.'

'I will take some home too,' said Gretel, and she filled the pockets of her pinafore.

Then Hansel said, 'We must find our way out of the forest. Come Gretel!'

Hand in hand, the two children set out and after walking for a long time they came, at last, to a vast stretch of water.

'We cannot cross without a boat,' said Hansel. 'And it is too far to swim.'

'Perhaps that gentle duck I see swimming towards us will help,' said Gretel, and she went down to the water's edge.

Then, stretching out her arms towards the duck, she called, 'Duck, Duck, will you help us to cross this water?'

The good little duck swam towards them and Gretel said, 'Here she comes, Hansel! Climb on her back and she will take you safely to the other side. Then she will fetch me.'

Just as Gretel had said, the duck carried first Hansel and then herself to the bank on the far side, and, after thanking her, the two children set out once again.

It seemed only a little while before Hansel spied a cottage among the trees and recognised it as their own.

'Gretel! Gretel!' he cried. 'We're home!'

At the sight of his long-lost children, the poor woodcutter, whose wife was now dead, was speechless with joy. As he hugged them to himself, Hansel said, 'We have something to show you, father!'

Well, you can guess what that something was — the witch's treasure! Diamonds, pearls and rubies glinted and glowed as Hansel and Gretel emptied their pockets.

Then the children told their story and the woodcutter listened with wondering eyes. When they reached the end of it, their father took them into his arms all over again.

'From now on!' he cried, 'we shall always be together, I promise you!'

And so they were and, with the help of the witch's treasure, they lived happily for a hundred years or more.

The Golden Goose

There was once a man who had three sons, two of whom were clever, while the third was extremely foolish. He was the youngest, and people called him Dummling or just plain fool.

The two clever sons were the light of their mother's eye, but not so poor Dummling who received no thanks for his work.

One day, the eldest brother went out into the forest to hew wood. Besides his axe, he took with him a fine piece of fruit cake and a bottle of red wine which his loving mother had given him before he set out.

He was no sooner in the forest and ready to cut down his first tree when he saw a little, old man with a grey beard watching him.

'Good-day to you,' said the stranger. 'I'm glad to see you for I'm desperately hungry and thirsty.'

'That's no business of mine,' retorted the eldest son rudely.

'I thought you would spare me a bite of that fruit cake you have in your rucksack and a drink of your wine,' went on the stranger.

'And if I did,' answered the young man, 'there would be far less for me when I've finished cutting down this tree. So be off with you!'

The little man turned away. But when the clever son set about hewing down the tree the axe slipped and cut his arm so badly that he left off work and returned home.

That same day, the second son went into the forest to finish his brother's work. And his loving mother gave him a slab of rich cake and a bottle of sweet wine.

He too saw the little old man with the greybeard and he too was asked to share his cake and wine.

'What!' he cried. 'You expect me to share my cake and wine with a stranger? Not on your life! Be off with you!'

The little man turned away. But when the clever son set about hewing down the tree, the axe slipped and cut his leg so badly that he left off work and limped all the way home.

'Let me go out and chop down that tree,' Dummling begged, as his mother fussed round his two brothers.

'You'll only end up cutting off your own head!' his mother retorted. And his father said, 'Oh, let him go! He'll learn his lesson when he cuts himself.'

Then his mother put a stale piece of bread in Dummling's rucksack and gave him a bottle of wine which had gone sour.

Now, when Dummling saw the little old man with the grey beard beside the tree, he smiled pleasantly and wished him good-day.

'Good-day to you,' replied the little old man. 'Can you spare me a bite to eat for I'm both hungry and thirsty?'

'You're welcome to all that I have,' said Dummling. 'It's not much for I've only got stale bread and sour wine.'

'That will do,' said the little man. But when Dummling himself took some of the bread it tasted like rich plum cake and the wine, too, was rich and sweet.

'Now,' said the stranger, when they had finished the cake and drunk the wine, 'I will do something for you. I will give you the gift of good luck for you have shown you have a kind heart.'

'What must I do for such a gift?' Dummling asked eagerly. And the little man pointed to an ancient tree some distance away.

'Cut down that tree,' he said, 'and you will find something at the roots.' Then he bade him good-day and vanished.

To his great surprise, when Dummling cut down the tree he found a goose sitting in the roots. The goose had feathers of purest gold and Dummling, on seeing this, made up his mind, there and then, to go out into the world and seek his fortune.

He tucked the goose under his arm, left the forest, and made his way to the nearest town. He asked for and got a room at the first inn he came to and, with the goose firmly tucked under his arm, went upstairs.

Full of high spirits, Dummling tethered the goose to his bed, then went out to look around.

Now the innkeeper had three daughters

and all three caught sight of the golden goose as Dummling carried it up to his room. And all three made up their minds to steal one of the golden feathers at the first opportunity.

The eldest daughter went to the room first, thinking, 'If I can just pluck one golden feather from that goose my dowry is assured.' And she took hold of the goose by its wing.

To her dismay she found her hand was stuck to the bird's golden feathers and no matter how she pulled she could not get free.

A few minutes later, the second sister crept into the room, but she had scarcely touched her sister when she too was held fast.

When the third and youngest sister came to the room, the other two screamed at her to go away. Too late, the young girl had already taken hold of her sister's dress and she too

was held fast. When Dummling returned home he found the three girls in his room and all four spent the night with the goose.

Dummling paid no attention to the girls in the morning, but set out with the goose under his arm and the girls were obliged to run after him. As Dummling walked through the town whom should he meet but the parson!

'Have you no shame running after a young man?' The parson shouted sternly, and he took hold of the last of the girls by the shoulder, so that he too was stuck fast. Away walked Dummling with the three girls and the parson tailing behind.

They had only gone a little way when they came to three labourers by the roadside.

'Help us!' screamed the parson, and the biggest of the labourers stumbled forward and took hold of the parson's black coat. He too was stuck fast. His mate took hold of his shoulder to pull him away and he too was held fast.

Then, the smallest of the labourers, thinking that he would be a hero, ran up but scarcely had he touched his companion's shoulder, then he too was held fast. So Dummling continued on his way with all seven following him.

He left the town far behind and walked on until he came to the city where the King had his palace. Now this King had a daughter who had never laughed, and the King had sent out a decree which said that whoever made his daughter laugh could marry her.

When Dummling heard this, he made his way quickly to the palace and into the royal presence. Doffing his cap, he paraded up and down in front of the Princess. At the sight of seven people running round and round, one behind the other, the Princess burst out into merry peals of laughter.

'You must keep your promise,' said Dummling to the King, 'I have made the Princess laugh and so you must give her to me in marriage.'

But the King had no liking for the young man who was dressed so poorly. He began to make excuses.

'There are one or two things you must do,' he said, 'before you can marry the Princess. First you must show me a man who can drink a whole cellarful of wine.'

Dummling's heart fell because he knew no man who could perform such a colossal task. But he remembered the little grey-bearded man who had first helped him.

'I will go back into the forest,' he told himself, 'and try to find him.' And as he made up his mind to do this the spell that had held the seven people broke and they were all free to return home.

With the golden goose still tucked under his arm, Dummling made his way back to the forest where he had felled the ancient tree and there, beside it, he saw a man with a very sad face.

'Whatever is the matter with you?' Dummling asked. 'You look miserable.'

And the man replied, 'I have such a great thirst that even fifty barrels of wine could not satisfy it.'

'I can help you to satisfy your thirst!' cried Dummling. 'Just come with me.' And he took the man into the King's cellar and showed him the great barrels of wine.

'There you are!' said Dummling. 'Now you can drink to your heart's content.'

The King was angry when he went into the cellar the next morning and found all the barrels of wine had been drunk.

'There is a second thing you must do,' he said to Dummling. 'You must find a man who can eat a whole hill of bread.'

Dummling's heart sank, but he went once again into the forest to the place where he had first felled the ancient tree. There he saw a man who was strapping himself up with a broad leather belt. 'Whatever are you doing?' Dummling asked.

And the man replied, 'I have eaten a whole sack of rolls but my hunger is still as great as ever. I am fastening this big strap round my stomach to stop myself from falling apart.'

'I can help you to satisfy your hunger,' said Dummling. 'Just come with me.' And he led the man to the King's bake-house where a whole hill of bread had been baked.

The thin man's face lit up with joy and he began to eat. By the end of the day, the hill of bread had disappeared.

For the third time Dummling went to the King and asked him for his daughter's hand.

'There is yet one more task which you must perform,' said the King. 'You must find me a ship which can sail on land *and* water.'

Dummling went straight back to the forest and there he found the little grey-bearded man whom he had first seen.

'You have a kind heart,' said the little grey-bearded man. 'You helped me once, now I will help you for the third time.' And he gave Dummling a ship which could sail on both land and water. When the King saw the ship come sailing over the courtyard towards his palace, he made up his mind at last to to give Dummling his daughter in marriage.

The two were married amidst great ceremony and Dummling and his wife lived happily ever afterwards. In the years to come Dummling became King, and no one in the kingdom remembered that once he had been known as a fool.

Rapunzel

There was once a man and a woman who had everything in their married life to make them happy except for one thing. They had no children.

The woman longed for a child so much that she could think of little else. Then one day it looked as if her dearest wish was going to be granted.

In her new-found happiness the woman would spend long hours at the sitting-room window which overlooked a wonderful garden filled with flowers and herbs.

No visitors ever came to this garden for it belonged to an enchantress who was feared by the whole town.

One day, when the baby was almost due to arrive, the woman looked down, as usual, into this wonderful garden and noticed a bed that was planted with the most tempting rampion.

'Husband, come quickly!' she called. And when he came, she pointed to the rampion and said, 'Just look at that rampion. I have so great a longing for it that I can almost feel the taste of it in my mouth.'

The husband, who loved his wife and tried

to give her everything she wanted, was immediately afraid.

'I dare not go to the enchantress and ask her for some of her rampion,' he said timidly. 'You know what they say about her.'

At this, his wife sighed deeply and kept her eyes fixed on the bed of rampion which was also known as rapunzel.

All through that day and the next, she went on about the rampion until at last her poor husband cried out in despair, 'Wife, you will have your rampion!'

When it was almost dark, the husband left the house and scaled the high stone wall that surrounded the witch's garden on three sides. Quickly he filled the basket he had brought with him with rampion, climbed back over the wall, and was in his own house all within a matter of minutes.

His wife was delighted. She made a salad with the rampion and ate it greedily. But, alas, the desire for the herb did not vanish. The next day she longed for more rampion. And once again the husband made his way over the high wall and into the witch's garden.

This time he was not so fortunate. Just as he was preparing to scale the wall with his prize, the enchantress came into the garden and caught him. 'Wicked thief!' she screamed at him, her eyes red and menacing. 'I will punish you. You will suffer for this deed.'

The poor man stammered out his explanation and so afraid was he that his legs would not bear his weight and he sank to the ground.

The old witch, seeing the fright he was in, said more quietly, 'You may take all the rampion you want on one condition. You must give me the child your wife will bear.'

The husband was so terrified that he gave his promise and the enchantress let him go free. But, shortly afterwards, when his wife had her child, the enchantress appeared and took the baby away from her.

The enchantress kept the baby girl in her own house, giving her the name of Rapunzel after the herb, and loving her as if she were her very own daughter.

The baby grew into a lovely young girl with eyes as blue as a summer sky and hair as fine and brilliant as spun gold.

When she was twelve, the enchantress shut her up in a high tower in the forest thinking that this was the way to keep the lovely young girl all to herself.

There were no doors or stairs to the turret but only a tiny window and whenever the old woman came to see Rapunzel, she stood beneath the tower window and called up:

'Rapunzel, Rapunzel,
Let down your hair to me.'

When Rapunzel heard these words, she undid her long braids of hair which were wound all about her head. Then she twisted them round the window post before letting them drop to the ground beneath so that she might pull up the enchantress.

Now, it came to pass, that the King's son happened to be in the forest and close to the tower when suddenly he heard the sound of singing. The voice was so clear and so sweet that he listened as if spellbound.

'It is coming from the tower, that is certain,' he told himself. But when he looked for a door or a stairway he could see neither the one nor the other.

But the Prince had lost his heart to the owner of the voice and day after day he guided his horse through the forest in the direction of the tower.

One day, to his surprise, he saw the old enchantress, though she did not see him, and he heard her call:

'Rapunzel, Rapunzel,
Let down your hair to me.'

From his hiding place, he saw the lovely face of Rapunzel at the turret window and then down came the long shining braids of golden hair, and up, up, went the witch until she disappeared from sight.

The handsome Prince could scarcely wait for darkness to fall. When it did, and the old woman had long since departed, he went to the foot of the tower and called:

'Rapunzel, Rapunzel,
Let down your hair to me.'

Almost at once two braids of shiny golden hair were cast down and grasping them in both hands the Prince climbed upwards.

At the sight of the young man, Rapunzel cried out in sudden fright, but then, the King's son knelt at her feet, vowing that he had never set eyes on any girl as beautiful as she.

And with soft words and gentle glances he brought a smile to her rosy lips.

'My old dame is the only mother I know,' Rapunzel told him. 'She will never, never set me free.'

'Then we must find a way,' said the Prince, 'for I love you with all my heart and wish to make you my wife.'

'I cannot use my own hair as a rope,' the girl told him, when he was preparing to take his leave. 'But if you brought a skein of silk with you each time you visited me, then I could weave the skeins into a ladder.'

'I will do that,' promised the King's son,

as Rapunzel prepared to drop her braids out
of the window.

The Prince came, as he had promised, each
night to see his future bride and each time
he brought with him a skein of silk.

In the daytime, after the enchantress had
gone, Rapunzel worked on her ladder.

One morning, the witch came as usual and
Rapunzel, whose thoughts were now always
on her Prince, exclaimed, 'Tell me, old Dame,
how is it that you are so much heavier than
the King's son to pull upwards?'

'Wicked child!' screamed the old woman, who guessed immediately what had been happening. 'You have fooled and tricked me!'

And in her anger she took hold of a pair of scissors and snipped off Rapunzel's long, shiny braids of golden hair.

Even then her anger grew no less and, with bitter words, she used her magic powers to transport Rapunzel into a vast, bleak desert where she left her.

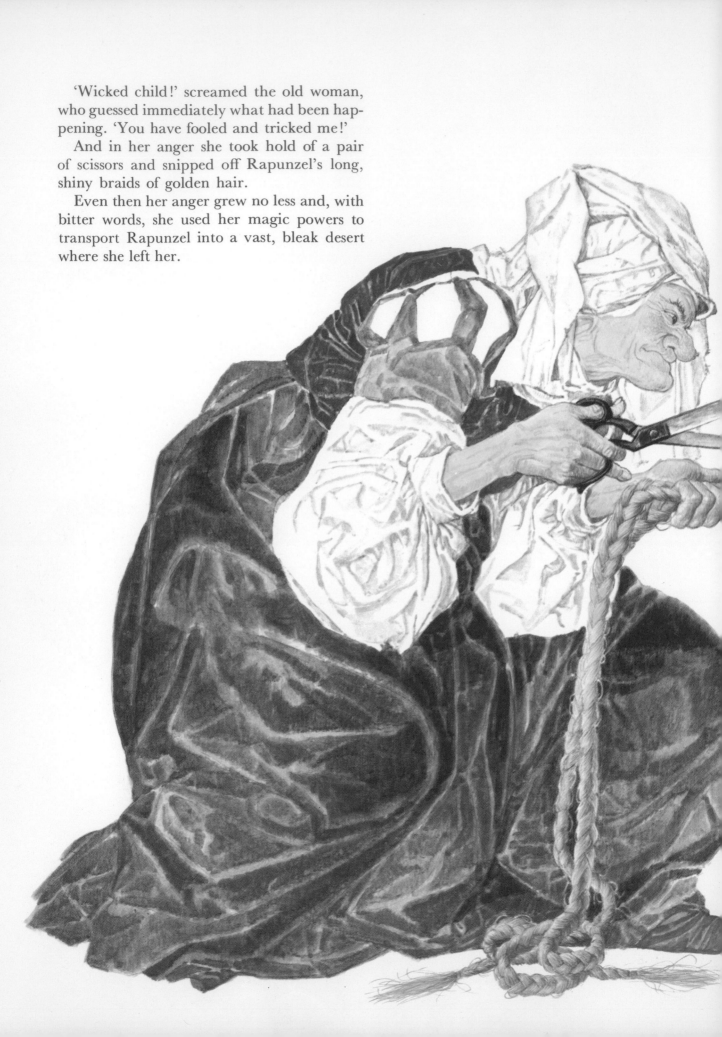

Then the enchantress returned to the tower to wait for the King's son.

He came, at last, just as night fell and, as usual, he called out:

'Rapunzel, Rapunzel,
Let down your hair to me.'

As soon as she heard the familiar words, the old witch threw down the golden braids, and the unsuspecting Prince began to climb upwards.

Imagine the Prince's horror when he found himself face to face with the enchantress, who cried mockingly, 'So you would take my daughter from me!'

There was no escape for him but to turn and jump from the high turret window and this he did. Down, down he fell, landing on a thorn bush whose cruel thorns pierced his eyes and left him blind.

Condemned to wander aimlessly, the Prince found no one to help him until, at last, his steps took him into the very desert where Rapunzel had lived alone for seven years.

With a cry of joy, Rapunzel recognised him and clasped him in her arms, her warm tears falling on his sightless eyes and giving them life.

With his sight restored, the Prince led Rapunzel out of the desert and back to his palace where they were married and lived in happiness for ever and for ever.

The Frog Prince

Once upon a time there was a good and wise King who had a very lovely daughter. The Princess was so pretty that poets vowed she was fairer than the fairest rose in the royal gardens.

Beyond these royal gardens, which were famous for their roses, lay the shady green forest. It was here, in the forest, that the Princess was most often to be found.

Day after day she would walk in the forest until she came to the fountain. Once there she would spend happy hours just throwing her golden ball high into the air and catching it again.

On one such day, the young Princess tossed her golden ball so high into the air that she failed to catch it again. Away it rolled and then disappeared from sight down a deep well close to the fountain.

The Princess cried out in dismay for she loved her golden ball better than she loved all her jewels and pretty dresses. As she began to weep and then loudly sob, there suddenly came a voice which said, 'Your sobs would melt the heart of a stone, my beautiful Princess.'

The Princess stopped crying and looked about for the owner of the voice but all she could see was a big fat ugly frog that had hopped out of the well on to a flat water-lily leaf.

'Don't mock me!' cried the Princess, in an angry voice. 'My beautiful golden ball has fallen into the well and I have lost it for ever.'

'Not so!' croaked the frog. 'I can jump into the well and bring it back to you. But if I do this you must give me something in return. I must have a reward.'

'You can have anything you want!' cried the Princess. 'I'll give you my new bracelet if you like or if you prefer you can have my very own golden crown which I will fetch from the palace.'

'No, no, I want none of these things,' said the frog.

'Then accept some golden florins which my father, the King, will let me have for you,' pleaded the Princess, 'only fetch my ball, I beg you.'

'I'll tell you what I want,' said the frog. 'I want to be your friend. I want to sit at table with you and eat out of your own golden dish and drink out of your own silver goblet. When I am tired I want you to carry me upstairs to your room and let me sleep in your own silken bed.'

The Princess was greatly surprised when she heard the frog speak in this way. Then she thought, 'Poof! It's only a frog and these are only silly, stupid words. It can't mean what it says. How could a frog expect to be my friend and eat off my plate and sleep in my silken bed?'

So aloud, she said, 'Yes, yes, I promise. Now fetch me my golden ball out of the well.'

As soon as the big frog heard the Princess give her promise, it hopped back to the well and dropped into the water.

The Princess waited and watched anxiously. Would the frog keep its promise? She didn't mean to keep hers but the frog couldn't know this and it had seemed very confident that it would find the ball.

The waters of the fountain splashed and glinted in the hot sun but today the young Princess had no eye for their beauty. All she could think about was her golden ball that was lost for ever.

dismay. 'I cannot run like you. Wait for me! Wait for me!'

But the Princess only ran all the faster. When she reached the palace she climbed the marble stairs up to her room because she did not wish her father, the King, to see that she was out of breath with running.

The next day she had forgotten all about the ugly frog by the well and the promise she had made it. But that night as she sat down to supper with the King and all his courtiers there came a soft knock at the door.

'There is someone at the door,' said the King. 'Daughter, you are the youngest at table; it is your duty to open the door. Pray do so.'

As he spoke, there came another knock at the door, and a harsh voice called out:

'Princess, dear Princess, let me come in!'

'Who can it be who calls you by name?' asked the King in surprise. 'Daughter, go at once and open the door.'

The Princess had recognised the frog's voice and would have disobeyed her father if she dared, but she dared not.

When she reached the door and opened it she saw, as she half expected, the big ugly frog and without a moment's thought hastily slammed the door in its face.

'Who was it that called you by name?' her father asked, as she slipped into her seat again.

'Nothing — nobody!' she answered.

'You look pale and you are trembling,' the King went on. 'What is it, child? What are you afraid of! What are you trying to hide from me?'

The Princess remained silent until the knocking came again.

'It's only a stupid ugly frog,' she mumbled at last.

'What can a frog want with a Princess?' her father asked in surprise.

And then the Princess was forced to tell the King the story of her lost ball and how she'd promised to befriend the frog and even

Then all at once she saw the frog's ugly head appear over the rim of the well and in a moment it was hopping towards her, holding the ball.

'You have got my golden ball!' the Princess cried in high delight. 'Give it to me! Give it to me!'

And when the frog was close enough, she bent down and snatched the ball from it with no word of thanks.

Then away she ran through the forest with never a backward glance at the frog.

'Princess! Princess!' croaked the frog in

let it eat out of her golden plate and sleep in her silken bed.

'A promise given must be kept, no matter at what cost,' said the King sternly. 'You must open the door and allow the frog to sit at table with you.'

When her father spoke sternly the young Princess dared not disobey him and so she went again to the door and opened it.

The frog hopped inside and followed behind her. Then it hopped up on to her chair and from there on to the table.

'Now push your plate near to me,' it said, 'so that I may share your food and eat with you as you promised.'

Pouting and near to tears, the Princess did so, but as the frog began to eat the Princess turned her head away.

At the end of the meal, which the frog seemed to enjoy, it said, 'Now, carry me up to your room and lay me down on your silken bed so that I may pass the night in your sweet company.'

The King nodded and the Princess picked up the frog distastefully and carried it up to her room.

'Now, place me on your pillow,' said the frog as soon as they were inside the dainty white-walled room.

'No! No! Never!' screamed the Princess, suddenly beside herself with rage. 'You are nothing but an ugly frog. How dare you ask such a favour!'

And with that, she lifted her arm and then hurled the frog against the wall.

As the frog struck the wall, his skin fell away. He was a frog no longer but a King's son — a handsome young Prince!

The Princess rubbed her eyes in amazement and the Prince said, 'I do not blame you, dear Princess, for the way you have treated me. I have been in the power of a wicked magician for seven years.'

'Did — did I help you to break the spell?' the Princess asked in a small, shamed voice.

'You did,' the Prince told her. 'You let me eat at your table and you carried me up to your room — no matter how unwillingly — and for that I thank you.'

At this the Princess began to smile for she was truly a nice girl at heart and so sweetly did she do this that the Prince knelt at her feet and begged her to marry him.

They were married in great splendour that very same week and the Princess left her own palace and went to live in the Prince's palace which was even grander than her own!

The Wishing-Table and the Goat

There was once a tailor who was more fond of his goat than his three sons.

This was chiefly because they counted on the goat for a regular supply of milk which was often all they had to keep body and soul together.

The sons had never worked, but took it in turn to lead the goat to the best pastures so that she might eat her fill.

One day, the eldest son took the goat to the churchyard where some very fine herbs grew in a wild state. He watched her eat her fill and just as night was falling, he asked, 'Goat, have you had enough to eat?'

The goat answered:
> 'I have eaten so much,
> Not a leaf more I'll touch!'

And she bleated in a contented fashion.

'Then I'll take you home,' said the eldest son, and he led her back to the barn and tied her up with a length of rope.

That night, at supper, the old tailor asked his eldest son if the goat had had enough to eat.

'Certainly, she has,' he replied. 'She has eaten so much that not a leaf more will she touch.'

But this did not satisfy the tailor and, after supper, he made his way to the barn to assure himself that all was well with his beloved goat.

'You're not hungry, are you?' he asked, as he stroked her coarse hair.

'Hungry!' replied the goat. 'Meh, meh, I didn't have a single bite the live long day. Meh, meh, of course I am hungry.'

This so upset and angered the old man that he ran back to the house, grabbed a stout stick and with blows and curses drove his eldest son into the night.

It was the turn of the second son to take the goat out the next day, and he found a corner in the meadow where there were lots of fine herbs and long, juicy grass.

The goat gobbled up everything in sight and when night was falling he asked her if she had had enough to eat.

The goat answered:
> 'I have eaten so much,
> Not a leaf more I'll touch.'

And she bleated in a contented fashion.

'Then I'll take you home,' said the second son and he led her back to the barn and tied her up with a length of rope.

That night, at supper, his father asked if the goat had had enough to eat.

'She has eaten so much,' his second son told him, 'that not another leaf will she touch.'

But when the old man went down to the barn to see for himself how the goat fared and ask her if she were still hungry, the goat replied, 'Hungry! Meh, meh, I didn't have a single bite the live long day. Meh, meh, of course I am hungry.'

Greatly upset, and furiously angry with his second son, the tailor ran back to the house, took up his cudgel and drove his second son into the night.

It was the turn of the third son next. And he made up his mind to do better than his two brothers. He led the goat farther afield to a place where he knew some bushes grew which had green, succulent leaves.

He watched the goat gobble up the leaves until all the bushes were stripped clean. Then he asked her if she had had enough to eat.

The goat answered:

'I have eaten so much,
Not a leaf more I'll touch.'

'Then I'll take you home,' said the third son, and he led her back to the barn and tied her up with a length of rope.

As soon as his father saw him, he asked if the goat had eaten her fill.

'She has eaten so much that not a leaf more will she touch,' his youngest son told him.

'I'll just see for myself,' said the old tailor, and he went down to the barn.

'You're not hungry, are you?' he said to the goat in a gentle voice.

'Hungry?' replied the goat. 'Meh, meh, I didn't have a single bite the live long day. Meh, meh, of course I am hungry.'

'Oh, what fools I have for sons!' cried the tailor in sudden anger. 'What lies they tell me!'

And he rushed into the house and with blows and curses drove his youngest son into the night.

Now that his sons were gone, the old man had to take the goat to pasture himself. And the very next morning, with many endearing words, he led his goat to a place where a leafy green hedge stretched for miles.

The goat ate greedily all day long and as night fell, the tailor took her back to the barn and tied her up.

Just as he was leaving the barn, the tailor exclaimed, 'Now, I *know* you are not hungry!'

But to his dismay, the goat said, 'Hungry! Meh, meh, I didn't have a single bite the live long day. Meh, meh, of course I am hungry.'

Scarcely able to believe his ears, the old man rushed back inside the barn and stood over the goat.

'You say you are hungry, but I know that it cannot be! I saw, with my own eyes, how you stripped the hedge.'

The goat said nothing, and the tailor went on in a voice shaking with rage. 'Miserable creature! I have lost my three sons because of you! You told the lies, not they!'

Then, he untied the goat and dragged her after him into the house.

'Now I'm going to teach you a lesson you will never forget,' raged the old man, and he fetched a razor and shaving soap.

'You shall be a bald-headed goat when I'm finished with you,' he muttered, as he began to shave the hair off the goat's head. 'No one will want you, and you will be driven this way and that.'

The goat submitted patiently to being shaved, but this did not soothe the tailor. When he had finished, he fetched out his horsewhip and with furious cries and much cracking of the whip drove the goat out of his house and his heart for ever.

Now, the tailor was all alone and, as the weeks and months passed, he grew more and more sad at the loss of his sons.

Meanwhile, the sons were doing very well for themselves.

The eldest had found a joiner who was more than willing to teach him his trade. At the end of his apprenticeship, his master brought out a little wooden table.

'It's not much to look at,' he said, 'but that doesn't matter, for this table is a wishing-table and I want you to have it.'

'What does it do?' asked the eldest son. And his master told him.

'Whenever you feel hungry, you must stand over it, utter the words, 'Little table, spread yourself!' and immediately there will be as much on the table as you can eat and drink.'

'That's a magnificent present,' said the eldest son gratefully. 'I'll take it home to my father.'

He had decided, you see, that after so many months, his father would have forgotten all about his anger and welcome him back.

With the little table tucked under his arm,

the eldest son set out for home, rejoicing in his good fortune.

The way was long and he had to pass through forests and meadows as well as towns, but he was never hungry or anxious about where his next meal was coming from. All he had to do was to set his little table down in front of him and utter the words, 'Little table, spread yourself!' And immediately, the good little table was covered with a white cloth and a plate was there and a knife, fork and spoon.

Then, whatever he had a mind to eat, be it roast beef or roast duck or boiled mutton, the plate was filled. And whatever wine went

best with the meal appeared to hand in a fine crystal goblet.

The last village before his own lay directly in his path, and the new young joiner made up his mind to stay the night at the local inn. It was late when he arrived and most of the guests had eaten.

'That doesn't matter at all,' he said, when the innkeeper told him this. And he put down his wishing-table and uttered the words, 'Little table, spread yourself.'

The guests watched in amazement as they saw the little table cover itself with a white cloth, knife, fork and spoon.

'I'll have a leg of pork and roast turkey,' the tailor's son said quietly, and his wish was granted at once.

'You're all welcome to join me,' said the young man. 'Sit down and help yourselves, those of you who are still hungry.'

Several of the travellers who had not been able to afford more than bread and cheese sat down immediately, and there was much talking and laughing as they began to eat.

Only the innkeeper remained silent as he watched from his corner.

'If I had such a table,' he thought to himself, as he saw how the empty plates filled up again, 'I would save myself the expense of paying a cook.'

Amid the cheers and grateful thanks of the guests, the joiner at last took his leave of them and went upstairs to bed.

He laid his wishing-table beside him as he climbed into bed and had no doubt at all that he would find it there in the morning.

But it was not to be, for whilst he slept the innkeeper went into his storeroom and found a table which was exactly like the wishing one. This, he took upstairs, and as stealthily as any thief in the night, crept into the joiner's room and exchanged the tables.

'He'll find out too late,' the innkeeper said to himself, as he stole away, 'and I'll see to it that he has a good breakfast before he begins his journey so that he will have no need to try out his table.'

The next morning, the joiner was delighted with the lavish breakfast the innkeeper put before him. And, after he had eaten it, he picked up his table and set out for home.

The old tailor was overwhelmed with joy at the sight of his long lost eldest son and,

after he had made him welcome, he began plying him with questions.

'How have you spent your time?' he asked him. 'Have you made your fortune?'

'I have never been hungry,' said his son, at last. 'And I'll never be hungry again and that's better than all the gold in the bank, I assure you.'

Then he told his father how he had become a joiner and how at the end of his apprenticeship, his master had given him a present.

'You don't mean it's that old wooden table you have under your arm?' his father asked at length.

'Oh, it looks ordinary enough, I admit,' replied the son, 'but you should see what it can do, when I speak to it.'

The old tailor looked at the table again. 'No matter what you say,' he began, 'it's not a table any one would put in their best room, now is it?'

'The best place for my table is in the kit-

chen,' said the young joiner with a loud laugh. 'Do you know, father, that if I set it down and tell it to spread itself, it will provide us with food fit for a King!'

Then, as his father shook his head in a very doubting way, his son cried, 'I tell you what — let's invite all our relatives round for a big feast. My wishing-table will provide all the food and wine for the party.'

Not liking to offend his son on his first day home, the tailor went round to all his relatives and friends and invited them back to his house. And when they were all gathered together, his son put the table down in front of him and said, 'Little table, spread yourself.'

But nothing happened. The table remained bare, and the guests began to laugh and mock the young man until he ran up to the attic and hid himself out of shame.

Meanwhile, the second son had found a miller who was willing to teach him his trade.

At the end of this apprenticeship, the miller said, 'You deserve a reward for having served me so well. I am going to give you a most unusual present.' And he went into his barn and led out an ass. 'Don't ask it to carry you,' said the miller, 'or draw a cart.'

'What shall I ask it to do then?' asked the former apprentice.

'Just say to it the magic word 'Bricklebrit', and the ass will let fall a shower of golden pieces, both from its front and its rear.'

'My, that's a magnificent present!' cried the young miller. 'I shall never know what it is to be poor. With such a creature I can keep my old father in comfort for the rest of his life.'

And with that, the tailor's second son led the ass away and set out for home for, like his brother, he was certain his father would long ago have forgotten his anger.

His journey was a most pleasant one. Whenever his pockets were empty, all he had to do was to take his ass into a quiet wood or field and speak the magic word, 'Bricklebrit' and

there was gold enough for a meal and a bed.

The miller came at last to the same inn that had sheltered his eldest brother, but when the innkeeper offered to take his ass and put it in the stable for the night, the miller shook his head. 'No thank you,' he said. 'I will look after the beast myself and see what stable it goes into.'

The innkeeper thought this was very odd but when he saw the young man pull out a purse of gold, he said nothing. Instead he made up his mind to double his charges for a meal and bed.

In the morning, the miller asked for his bill in advance but, on seeing the amount, he said, 'Wait here. I'll be back in a trice.'

The innkeeper's small, greedy eyes grew sharp as he watched the young man go into the yard and enter one of the stables.

'There must be something rare and precious inside that stable,' he thought to himself, as he heard the door of the stable shut. 'Why does he take such care?'

And moving as lightly as he could for his size, he tiptoed into the yard, knelt by the stable door, and put his eye to the keyhole.

What he saw completely amazed him, for there was the ass raining down gold pieces from both ends.

'If I had such a gold-mine in my possession,' the innkeeper thought, 'I could give up this inn and build myself a castle and live like a gentleman.'

Then the innkeeper remembered that he had a grey ass which was similar to the beast in the stable.

'It will take only a moment to switch the beasts over,' he decided, as he hurried back to the inn.

When the miller returned, he paid his bill from a purse stuffed with gold before sitting down to a sumptious breakfast.

'Eat your fill,' said the innkeeper, with a sly smile. 'There's no need to hurry.'

Whilst the miller was enjoying his breakfast, the innkeeper went back to the stables

The innkeeper watched him go to the stable and bring out the ass. But so similar was it to his own that the miller had no suspicion of the trick that had just been played upon him, and he went off down the road with a cheerful smile on his face.

The old tailor was overwhelmed with joy at the sight of his second son.

'It does my eyes good to see you again,' he said. 'Now, tell me, what trade did you learn whilst you have been away from home?'

'I apprenticed myself to a miller,' said his son. 'And at the end of my apprenticeship he made me a gift.'

And he took his father into the yard and showed him the ass.

'Well, it's a stout enough animal, to be sure,' said his father, 'and no doubt we can find a use for it.'

'It won't draw a cart,' replied his son.

'Then what will it do?' asked his father.

'It will make us rich beyond our dreams!' cried the young miller, 'for as soon as I say the magic word, 'Bricklebrit', it will shower us with gold.'

When the old tailor heard this, he threw up his hands in disbelief and his son put his arm round the ass's neck and said, 'I tell you, father, it is true. Let us ask all our relatives to come to our house. We can make their fortunes as well as our own.'

'You must be serious,' said the old man, beginning to jig up and down. 'I believe you now! Just think! I never need to patch or sew again.'

And he ran out and called all his relations. When they were gathered in one room, his son brought in the ass, spread a cloth at its feet and said, 'Bricklebrit,' very loudly.

Nothing happened! The tailor's son tried again, 'Bricklebrit! Bricklebrit!' shouted he, at the top of his voice, 'Bricklebrit!'

Still nothing happened, and his relatives and friends exploded into laughter.

'All right, all right,' said the old man, 'the joke has gone far enough. You can all go

and changed over the asses. Then, satisfied with his morning's work, he returned to his guest.

'That was one of the finest breakfasts I've enjoyed for a long time,' said the tailor's second son, as he wiped his mouth. 'Now, I must be on my way for I hope to be with my father before the end of the day.'

home.' But he was inwardly so ashamed and disappointed that he would not speak to his son, and went off to bed.

Meanwhile, the tailor's third and youngest son found a turner who was willing to teach him to work at the lathe.

Learning to be a lathe-worker was very hard, and the third son took a long time to become an expert. He began writing letters home and was delighted one day to receive a letter from his father telling him of his two brothers and the terrible disappointment over the wishing-table and the ass.

'No doubt the innkeeper cheated them,' his father had written, 'but there is no way to prove such a thing.'

When the youngest son at last completed his apprenticeship, his master presented him with a cudgel.

'It's not much after such hard work,' the

new turner thought to himself, but he didn't speak his thoughts aloud, which was just as well, for his master said, 'This is not just an ordinary cudgel, you know!'

'What is extraordinary about it?' asked the young man, as he dropped it into a sack.

'I'll tell you,' said his master. 'Whenever you are in trouble or in danger, perhaps of being robbed, all you have to say is, 'Out of the sack, cudgel', and the cudgel will leap out of the sack and beat your attacker until he is ready to drop.'

'That *is* extraordinary!' cried the tailor's son, 'And I suppose the cudgel will leap back into the sack when ordered to?'

'Exactly,' said the turner.

'Then I am most grateful to you for your gift,' said the young man.

On his journey homeward, the new turner had good reason to be grateful to his magic

cudgel for on more than one occasion he was set upon by robbers. Each time, on the word of command, the cudgel would leap out of the sack and, with many hard, swift blows, drive off the attackers.

When, at last, the young turner came to the inn where his brothers had been cheated, he put his sack on the table and began to talk to the innkeeper.

'Yes, yes,' he said, 'I have heard of a great many weird and wonderful things in my time; I have even heard talk of an ass that showers gold and a table that provides food fit for a King, but there is nothing in the whole world to equal the treasure I carry in this sack.'

'What is it? What can it be?' the greedy innkeeper asked himself as he listened. 'I think it must be diamonds and pearls or a crown, perhaps studded with rubies.'

That night, he showed the young turner where he could sleep, but he did not go to bed himself for he meant to steal the sack and keep its contents.

The turner used the sack for a pillow and pretended to fall asleep at once. But when the fat innkeeper attempted to pull the sack away, he sat up immediately.

'Out of the sack, cudgel!' commanded the young man, and the cudgel leapt out of the sack and set upon the unhappy thief.

'Mercy! Mercy!' cried the innkeeper, as the cudgel beat him about the back and the head. 'I meant no harm!'

'You are a liar and a thief!' exclaimed the turner, 'and my cudgel will go on beating you until you confess.'

The innkeeper tumbled off the bench and fell to the ground under the cudgel's blows, and the turner went on, 'What about the two things you stole from my brothers? Give me back the table that spreads itself and the ass that rains gold.'

'Anything! Anything!' screamed the poor innkeeper, 'Just stop this fiendish cudgel from beating me.'

At this, the turner said quietly, 'Cudgel, get into the sack.' And the cudgel left off beating the innkeeper and flew back into the sack. Then the turner waited whilst the innkeeper scrambled to his feet and went off to get the wishing-table and the ass.

'Let this be a lesson to you,' said the tailor's son severely, as he prepared to go. 'If you ever again rob a single guest, I will return with my cudgel.'

The turner then left the inn and made his way towards his own village where he knew he would find not only his father but his two brothers as well.

As he approached his house, the old tailor ran out to greet him and his two brothers put their arms round him and embraced him warmly.

'You are the last of my sons to come home,' said the tailor, smiling. 'Tell me what you have been doing.'

'I've been learning to be a turner,' said the young man, 'and at the end of my apprenticeship, my master made me a gift for he was well pleased with my work.' And he took out his cudgel and showed it to his father.

His father looked disappointed and on seeing this, the turner laughed. 'I know what you are thinking,' he said, 'but with this magic cudgel I have rescued both the wishing-table that spreads itself and the ass that rains gold at both ends.'

And he took his father to the little wood where he had hidden the ass and the table before entering the village.

'Now you will see if I did not speak truly about my table!' cried the eldest son.

'And you will see if I did not speak truly about my ass!' cried the second son.

And they ran off to invite all their friends and relations to come to the house immediately.

When they were all gathered together, the joiner fed them from his wonderful table and the miller filled their pockets with gold by means of his precious ass.

Then the old tailor put away his needle and cotton for good and prepared himself to live a life of ease for the rest of his life.

As for the goat — she was so ashamed of her bald head that she hid herself in a fox's hole and would have stayed there for ever if the fox had not asked the little bee to help him to get rid of her.

The bee stung the miserable goat on her bald patch which was too much to bear. With a loud 'Meh, meh!' she bolted out of the hole and into the forest and was never seen again by either man or beast.

King Thrushbeard

There was once upon a time a proud and haughty Princess who turned away one suitor after the other.

One day, her father, the King said, 'I am going to hold a great banquet and invite the richest and wisest men from many lands. You must choose a husband from among them.'

'I will certainly look them over,' replied the Princess who, by the way, was extremely beautiful, 'but I won't make any promises.'

On the day of the banquet all the young men who had been invited were asked to stand in line.

There were Kings and grand-dukes and earls and barons and wise scholars. Not all of them were handsome but all were known to be kind and good-mannered.

The Princess inspected them all with great thoroughness. Then she cried, 'This one is much too fat! And this one is far too thin. And just look at that one — he has nobbly knees!'

She went on in this rude manner until at last she spied a tall handsome man who wore a crown. 'And who may this be?' she enquired in a laughing way. 'I see he is a King but I see too that the beard on his chin has grown somewhat crookedly. I shall give him a special name — King Thrushbeard — for he has a chin like a thrush's beak.'

The Princess laughed loudly and then moved on down the long line, growing more and more rude as she went.

This made her father, the King, so angry and ashamed that at last he cried out, 'Stop! You shall be punished for your rudeness. I vow before all present that you will marry the first beggar who comes to my door.'

Some days after the banquet a poor, ragged fiddler came to the palace and began to play under the windows. When the King heard him, he said, 'Bring that fiddler inside. He will marry my daughter according to my vow.'

In vain the proud Princess protested, 'I won't wed such a miserable, ragged fellow!' she screamed.

'I have given my royal word before the entire court,' said the King. 'It cannot he broken. This beggar-man will be your husband and the wedding will take place at once.'

After the ceremony, the King looked at his disagreeable daughter and said, 'You are now a beggar's wife. It is not very fitting that you should remain here.'

Now the Princess had always lived at the palace and enjoyed every luxury that you would expect. The idea of going out into the world with a beggar for a husband threw her into such a rage that her face became quite ugly.

But the King was determined to have his way and the very next day the Princess and the beggar left the palace.

The fiddler took her by the hand and pulled her along after him. He was tall and strong and had a tongue as sharp as her own.

After walking a good distance they came, at last, to a huge forest and the Princess asked, 'Who owns this forest; it is very large?'

The beggar laughed and answered, 'This forest which stretches as far as the eye can see belongs to King Thrushbeard. If you had taken him for your husband the forest would have been all yours.'

The Princess sighed and murmured, 'Oh, what a foolish girl I was. I turned down so many fine suitors and now look what I have got for a husband!'

'You were too hard to please,' her husband told her. 'It is known all over the kingdom how you laughed at those who came to ask for your hand in marriage.'

The Princess walked on in silence until they came to a wide, rich meadow. 'Who owns this big meadow?' she asked.

'The meadow belongs to King Thrush-beard,' said the beggar. 'If you had taken him for a husband it would have been yours.'

'Alas,' the Princess sighed, 'what a fool I was to make fun of him and send him away.'

After walking a few more miles they came to a large town and once again the Princess asked a question. 'That's a fine big town,' she said. 'To whom does it belong?'

'The town with its tall buildings belongs to King Thrushbeard,' her husband told her. 'If you had taken him for a husband it would have been yours.'

'Alas,' the Princess sighed, 'what a fool I was to make fun of him and send him away.'

'That's enough,' said the beggar in a very gruff, angry voice. 'I am growing tired of your sighs and I don't want to hear another word about this King Thrushbeard. You are

my wife now and you belong to me.'

The Princess remained silent until they had gone through the town. But when her husband stopped before a small mean house, she could hold her tongue no longer and cried out, 'My, what a dreadful little house. It's so small that it would fit into my palace bedroom.'

'This is my house,' said the beggar, 'and this is where we shall live together.'

As the Princess entered the house, which in truth, was nothing more than a hut, she asked, 'Where are the servants? I cannot manage without servants.'

'Then you had best learn,' said her new husband with a laugh. 'You are a beggar's wife, don't forget! Now fetch some water from the well and set about cooking something for our supper.'

The days that followed were a nightmare for the Princess. She burned the pans and scalded her fingers and there was scarcely ever anything nice to eat.

At last her husband, who constantly jeered at her efforts, said, 'You will never make a good housewife. You had better try and earn me some money by spinning.'

But the Princess was as hopeless at spinning as she was at cooking.

'What a poor creature you are,' her husband remarked one evening. 'I have made a very bad bargain indeed!'

Then he brought out some pots which he had made himself and told her, 'I think you had better try and sell these earthenware pots.'

'What!' exclaimed the Princess, 'go into the market! Some of my father's courtiers might see me . . . can you imagine how they would all laugh!'

'I can,' said the beggar. 'But you are my wife and bound to obey me.'

So the next day the proud Princess found herself in a corner of the market surrounded by pots and pans.

To her surprise she managed to sell quite a few for she was still extremely pretty and people were attracted by her beauty.

For once, her husband praised her when she returned home with the money she had earned.

'You must go again tomorrow,' he said.

In the morning, the fiddler loaded himself up with a fresh lot of earthenware, some of which he had bought.

When they reached the market-place, he sat her down among all the goods and left her.

The Princess began selling her wares almost at once after she had moved to a busier spot, when suddenly a horseman, shouting and singing, came at a gallop through the market-place.

Even before the Princess had time to cry out his high-spirited horse had crashed into her wares and smashed them to smithereens.

At the sight of so much damage, the poor Princess buried her face in her hands and began to weep. 'My husband will beat me,' she moaned. 'What can I tell him!'

Certainly it would be hard to explain that she had moved herself and her goods to a busy corner of the market-place instead of staying where he had left her.

But, in the end, there was nothing else left to do but to go home and confess.

'Nothing you do turns out to be right,' said her husband. 'What a misfortune to be married to somebody like you. Well, there's nothing else for it. You must go back to the palace . . .' The Princess looked at her husband hopefully, but then he added, 'as a kitchen-maid. I have spoken to the chef and he will take you on.'

In vain the Princess pleaded against such a plan, but her husband would not give way and so, in the morning, she became a kitchen-maid in her own palace.

As kitchen-maid she had to do all the very meanest tasks in the vast kitchens and each night she returned to her husband with grimy cracked hands and a dirty face.

Now it happened that the King's eldest son was to be married and on the wedding day the Princess could not stop herself from wanting to see the ceremony. So she stole away from the kitchen and crept upstairs.

Hiding behind a cupboard, she watched the guests, all richly clad, take their place in the royal banqueting hall. And as she watched she began to wish with all her heart that she could have been among them. 'If only I had been gracious instead of cruel,' she thought, 'humble instead of proud, I might have been a welcome guest at my own brother's wedding.'

As she stood there, trembling, one of the guests, taller and more handsome than any of the other young men present, came up to her and dragged her from her hiding-place.

To her shame and horror, the Princess saw that it was King Thrushbeard. In vain, did she try to pull herself away; but the King persisted in drawing her into the hall.

'Dance with me,' he said gently.

'No, no,' protested the Princess. 'They will only mock me! How can a scruffy little kitchen-maid dance with a king!'

Already they were surrounded by guests and, as the Princess struggled, they began to laugh at her appearance.

With one final wrench, the Princess tore herself away from the King and fled.

As she reached the narrow back-stairs that led down into the kitchens, who should bar her way but the same King Thrushbeard!

Catching hold of her arm, the King said, 'I want you to listen to me.' And there was something in his voice which reminded her of — can you guess — the fiddler!

Then the King said, 'The beggar you so unwillingly married and the King standing before you are one and the same. I fell in love with you when we first met, but could see no way to tame your proud spirit except by disguising myself as a beggar.'

Then the Princess wept and whispered that she had indeed learned her lesson. The King told her they would be married all over again — which indeed they were — and never had the Princess looked more lovely than she did on her second wedding day!

The Shoemaker
and the Elves

There was once upon a time a poor but very honest shoemaker.

One day, through no fault of his own, he found he had no money left and only one small piece of leather.

'We shall go hungry soon,' he told his wife that night, 'for I have leather enough for only one pair of shoes.'

'Don't upset yourself, husband,' replied his wife. 'Just cut out the leather and come to bed. We'll say our prayers and hope for the best.'

So the shoemaker cut out the last piece of his leather, left it on his work-bench, and went upstairs to bed.

Imagine his surprise when he found a pair of finely made shoes all ready and waiting for him in the morning. He could scarcely believe his eyes as he looked at the expert stitching.

'I'll very soon sell these,' he thought to himself, and he did — for twice as much as he would have asked for in the usual way.

With the money, the shoemaker was able

to buy more leather for two more pairs of shoes. That night he cut out two pairs of shoes and left the leather on his work-bench.

In the morning, to his surprise and joy, he found two pairs of beautiful shoes and so fine was their workmanship, that he had no trouble in selling them that same morning.

With the money, the good shoemaker was able to buy more leather — enough to make three pairs of shoes — and that night he cut out the shoes and left the leather on the bench.

In the morning, he wasn't really surprised to find three pairs of fine shoes which he sold long before dinner.

And so it went on. Every morning, the shoemaker found his work done for him.

'We are very blessed,' said his wife one day, as they counted all their savings. 'We must have guardian angels working for us!' and she laughed happily.

'I would like to know how they became such skilled shoemakers,' chuckled her husband.

'I tell you what,' said his wife, 'let's sit up tonight and see for ourselves what is happening in our workshop.'

So that night the couple hid thmeselves in the room and waited until at last it was twelve o'clock.

The old woman yawned and was just about to ask her husband to come to bed when suddenly two undressed elves appeared.

As the couple watched, one picked up the leather and the other grasped one of the shoemaker's tools. Soon they were hard at work and the pile of shoes grew and grew.

The two merry little cobblers laughed and sang as they worked and when all the leather was used up, they ran quickly away.

The shoemaker could hardly find words to express his astonishment. But soon his wife was saying how wonderful it all was and how she longed to give the elves a nice present.

'I tell you what, husband,' she said, when they were back in their bedroom. 'It's going to be Christmas in another few days. I'll make these two little fellows a fine suit of clothes each. They'll like that!'

The next few days were very busy ones for the shoemaker's wife. She made vests and shirts and coats and she knitted socks — all a very tiny size. And when everything was ready the shoemaker carried them down to his bench and left them in a neat pile.

That night, the couple crept down just as midnight was striking. To their delight they saw that the two elves were already dressed in all their new clothes.

Then one began singing:
'Now we're proper boys at last,
All our cobbling days are past!'

Leaving the leather just where it was they skipped away out of the window.

And that was the last the cobbler and his wife ever saw of the two fairy cobblers. But they were so comfortably off by this time that they never worried again about being poor.

Snow-White and Rose-Red

In a little cottage at the very edge of a deep forest lived a poor widow woman with her two daughters.

The cottage was tiny but it did have a patch of garden in which grew two rose trees, one white and the other red. And the widow, who loved her roses, named her daughters after them. She called them Snow-White and Rose-Red.

Snow-White and Rose-Red grew up in a gentle, loving way — always kind and thoughtful to their mother and to each other.

In the summer they went into the forest to gather berries and firewood and sometimes to

play among the tall green trees. And in the winter, when snow covered the ground, they sat at their mother's feet with their pet lamb on the mat beside them listening to her stories of long ago.

In this manner, the years passed until one dark winter's night someone knocked on the door.

'Let me go,' said Snow-White, jumping up. And her mother said, 'Perhaps some traveller has lost his way in the snow.'

It was no traveller who stood there when Snow-White opened the door, but a huge brown bear!

Snow-White screamed in fright and quickly tried to shut the door. But the bear called out, 'Do not be afraid. I will not harm you. I am cold and hungry and seek only shelter for the night.'

'Poor bear!' said the widow, going to the door and opening it wide. 'You are white with snow. Do please come inside and make use of our fire.'

'When Snow-White and Rose-Red saw that the big bear meant them no harm they went up to him as he lay before the fire and brushed the snow out of his long hair.

Then the mother brought some honey and the bear lapped it up and seemed content to stay there for the whole of the night.

Snow-White and Rose-Red quickly lost all fear of the bear and they played with him and rolled him over and teased him; and the bear accepted all the teasing and fun with the greatest good nature. But as soon as day dawned the bear called Snow-White from her bed and she got up and opened the door and let him go.

All through the long winter the bear came each night and Snow-White and Rose-Red grew to love him and look forward to his visits.

'You are our friend,' they told him, over and over again. 'We shall always love you.'

But when spring came, the bear said, 'Now I must go away. You will not see me again for I must go into the forest and guard my treasure from the wicked dwarfs.'

'Where are they and why do we never see them?' asked Snow-White.

'The dwarfs hide under rocks and in caves,' said the bear. 'But in winter, when the earth is frozen, they must stay underground. It is only in the summer that they try to steal my treasure.'

Snow-White and Rose-Red were sad to see their friend go and Snow-White said, 'Maybe we shall meet you in the forest one day and then we can be together again for a short while.'

After the bear had gone and the two girls had tidied the cottage for their mother, they were free to play in the garden or walk in the forest.

'Let's go to the forest,' said Rose-Red. 'The bear has left us but the forest is green and the birds are singing. We will never feel sad in the forest.'

They had only gone a little way when all at once they saw something jumping up and down in the grass.

'What can it be?' Snow-White asked. 'It's extremely small. Let's go and see.'

When they drew near they saw that it was a dwarf with a creased-up face and sharp eyes. They saw, too, that his long white beard was caught in the crevice of a tree trunk so that he could not pull himself free.

As they stood wondering what they could do to help, the little man looked up.

'Don't just stare!' he screamed. 'Can't you see what has happened to me? What a pair of idiots you are. Help me!'

'We were wondering what to do for the best,' Rose-Red explained. 'Your beard is well and truly caught.'

'We could always try and pull you free,' said Snow-White doubtfully, 'but it might be painful, you know.'

'Stop talking and get on with it,' replied the dwarf.

'Very well,' said Rose-Red, who had a very kind heart and always wanted to help any one in trouble. 'We'll do our best.'

And she took hold of the little man by the waist and began to tug.

'Stop it! Stop it!' yelled the little man

after only a moment. 'You stupid girl! You are making my head ache.'

'I — I know what to do,' said Snow-White, and she took out a pair of scissors from her pocket. 'If we cut his beard we can set him free.'

'Don't you dare touch my beautiful beard!' screamed the dwarf, red in the face with anger.

'Then you will have to stay where you are,' replied Rose-Red, 'for it is your beard that is keeping you a prisoner.'

When the dwarf did not answer, Snow-White bent over him, and snip, snip she cut his beard.

'There you are,' she said, beginning to smile. 'You have only lost a tiny bit of your beard and you are free.'

But before she had finished speaking the little man was hopping up and down with rage.

'Fool!' he screamed at her. 'Look what you have done. You have left the best of my beard in that tree trunk.'

'My sister has set you free,' said Rose-Red gently, 'but for her you would still be a prisoner.'

'But for her I would still have all my beard,' retorted the dwarf nastily. And he stumped away from them.

As they watched, they saw him pick up a sack, which was filled to over-flowing with gold pieces, and drag it away.

'What a horrid little man,' said Rose-Red. 'He didn't give us one word of thanks for all the trouble we took.'

'Let's hope we never see him again,' said Snow-White. 'If there are any more in the forest like him, I won't feel like coming here.'

But the next day was so beautiful that their mother suggested they go into the forest again and enjoy the sunshine.

'You could take your fishing rods,' she said, 'And see if you can catch a fish for dinner.'

'At least we won't be going to that part of the forest where we met the dwarf,' Rose-Red said, as they made their way to the stream.

As they drew near, they saw through the trees what looked like a giant grass-hopper struggling in the air.

'Gracious!' Rose-Red exclaimed. 'Look, over there, Snow-White! Whatever is it?'

'Let's find out,' said Snow-White, and together they ran forward.

To their surprise and dismay, they found themselves staring at the dwarf.

'What are you doing?' asked Rose-Red, and she tried not to smile, for the little man looked very funny. 'Is anything wrong?'

'Fool!' snapped the tiny man, in the angry voice they had come to expect from him. 'Use your eyes! Can't you see that what's left of my beautiful white beard is all twisted up with my fishing line. And what's more — there's a beastly fish at the end of it trying to pull me in and drown me.'

'So there is!' said Rose-Red, peering down into the water. 'But how can we help, I wonder?'

'I'll try and pull you free,' offered Snow-White, and she took hold of the dwarf by the waist and began to pull him towards her. But the dwarf's beard was twisted so firmly round the fishing line that it did not budge an inch.

This time, Rose-Red got out her scissors. 'I'm sorry,' she said, 'but if you don't want us to leave you here, you will simply have to agree to having your beard cut.'

And with that, snip, snip went her scissors, and the dwarf dropped on to the bank.

'You'll get no thanks from me,' he cried, as he hopped away from them. 'You've spoilt what was left of my beautiful beard and I'll pay you back one fine day.'

As they watched, they saw him take a sack of pearls that lay half-hidden in the rushes and drag it behind a big stone.

Soon after this, their mother asked them to go to the village to get some things for her. So, once again, Snow-White and Rose-Red found themselves in the forest.

'I wonder what trouble our dwarf is in today?' Rose-Red laughed, as they ran along.

'Don't laugh,' said kind-hearted Snow-White, as they reached the clearing. 'Look, there he is and he seems terrified. Why does he keep looking up at the sky?'

As she spoke, something dark and menacing swooped down on the cringing dwarf.

'Quick!' Rose-Red cried. 'It's an eagle and already it has got its talons into the dwarf's coat. It's going to carry him off!'

They sprang forward and were only just in time to catch hold of the dwarf. Then it became a tug-of-war between themselves and the strong eagle.

'We've won!' Snow-White suddenly shouted, as the eagle, growing tired of the game, released its hold and soared away into the sky.

'Clumsy idiots!' muttered the dwarf. 'My good red coat is in shreds now!' And without a word of thanks he went over to a sack of precious stones which was lying on the ground and dragged it into a hole in the rocks.

On the way home, Snow-White and Rose-Red could not resist talking about the dwarf.

'There's the tree trunk where we first saw him!' said Snow-White suddenly. 'I wonder where he is now?'

They had only taken a few more steps when they got their answer. For there, in a clearing, was the dwarf himself and he was peering down at a carpet of rubies and diamonds and pearls spread out on the green grass.

The sun on the precious stones made them shine like stars, and the two sisters were fascinated.

'How beautiful!' Snow-White whispered, taking hold of her sister's hand. 'How did the dwarf come by such a treasure?'

Before Rose-Red could reply, the little man glanced up and saw them.

'So it's you again!' he shouted, his face turning red with anger. 'Spying on me now!'

Snow-White and Rose-Red shrank back, as the dwarf moved towards them.

'We — we weren't spying,' Snow-White stammered. 'We were on our way home to our cottage.'

'Interfering, meddlesome pair!' raged the dwarf, tugging at what was left of his white beard. 'You ruin my beautiful beard, and

now you would try to steal my treasures.'

Before he could go on, however, there came a loud fierce growl from the direction of the trees and a huge brown bear lumbered into the clearing.

With a scream of fright, the dwarf darted towards a hole in the rock, but the bear put out his great paw and pinned him to the ground.

'Spare me, Lord Bear!' whimpered the dwarf. 'If you eat me I will only be a morsel in your mouth. Eat these girls instead. See how plump they are!'

For answer, the bear lifted the struggling dwarf high into the air and then dashed him to the ground.

Then he turned to the sisters. 'Do not be afraid,' he said. 'Come closer and you will find that I am your old friend, the bear, who came to you all through the long months of winter.'

Snow-White took a step forward and as she did so the bear's skin fell from him. Instead of a huge brown bear there now stood a tall handsome young man robed like a Prince.

Smiling, the Prince told the two sisters his story. 'Long ago,' he began, 'whilst I was hunting in this very forest I stumbled upon the dwarf's hide-out and all the treasure he and his tribe had been looting from our palace. But, alas, I was no match for the evil leader of the dwarfs who now lies dead. He cast a spell on me before I left the forest and changed me into a bear.'

'Poor bear!' Snow-White cried. 'How glad I am we took you in and gave you shelter when the snow was on the ground.'

'Only the dwarf's death could break the spell,' the Prince continued, 'and now that this has come about the power of the dwarfs is destroyed for ever, and all their treasure will be restored to me.'

'Now that you are a Prince once again,' Rose-Red said, 'you will not want to come to our humble cottage.'

'That is not so,' said the Prince, and he turned and looked at Snow-White whose golden hair glinted in the sunshine.

'Will you come back with us now?' asked Snow-White, a pink flush on her cheeks. 'It would make us very happy if you would.'

'Indeed I will,' answered the Prince, taking her hand, 'for there is something I would say to your mother.'

Laughing and talking, all three made their way back to the cottage where once again the Prince told his story.

Then he said, 'And now, one thing more, I would like to ask for Snow-White's hand in marriage for I love her with all my heart.'

The widowed mother readily gave her permission, and the Prince took Snow-White back with him to his palace where they were married the very next day.

Amidst all the rejoicing, Snow-White found time to whisper to her mother and sister that it was her dearest wish they should leave the cottage and come and stay at the palace. And to this, they readily agreed.

And very soon afterwards, the Prince's twin brother fell in love with Rose-Red and made her his wife.

The two gentle sisters spread happiness all over the palace and throughout the kingdom, but none was happier than their own dear mother.

She found her greatest joy in just sitting at the window of her royal chambers gazing down into the garden at two rose trees — one red and one white — the very same that had once bloomed in her humble cottage garden.

Lucky Hans!

There was once upon a time a young man whose name was Hans. As soon as he was old enough to work, he hired himself out to a farmer and served him well and faithfully for seven years.

At the end of the seven years, Hans said to the farmer, 'I have served you well for the time we agreed. Now, I would like to go back to my mother. Will you give me my wages for my seven years of service?'

'I will play fair with you,' said the farmer, 'for you have been a good worker.' And he gave Hans a lump of gold as big as a turnip.

Hans wrapped the gold in an old sack and set off for his village which was a good day's walk away.

The sun was hot overhead as he tramped along, and very soon the gold began to weigh him down.

Hans wiped his forehead and sighed at the awful thought that he would have to carry his burden for so many miles.

Just then a horseman came trotting down the road on a big black horse. When he saw Hans, he called out, 'It's a fine day but by the looks of you, you won't agree!'

'It's all very well for you,' replied Hans, 'up there on your horse. But not for me — weighed down by this burden.'

'What is it?' asked the horseman, as he drew up beside Hans.

'It's a lump of gold,' said Hans, 'as big as a turnip and ten times as heavy.'

'I tell you what!' cried the horseman, getting down from his horse. 'Why don't we do an exchange? I'll take the gold and you take my horse. Then we'll both be happy.'

'Done!' cried Hans. 'I've always wanted to ride, and that's a very grand horse.'

'Then up you get,' said the horseman. And he hoisted Hans into the saddle.

Hans gathered up the reins. 'There's just one thing more,' he said. 'How do I make it go fast? I'm in a hurry to be home and see my mother.'

'Just cluck your tongue,' the stranger told him. 'It's simple.' And he went off down the road in the opposite direction.

In high delight, Hans walked his horse for a mile or two, and then clucked his tongue to make it go faster.

Away galloped the horse at a terrifying speed. Hans clung on as best as he could until the horse, seemingly anxious to let him see who was master, suddenly reared up. This was too much for Hans who lost his seat and toppled out of the saddle.

Nearly scared out of his wits at the unexpected turn of events, Hans was much relieved when a farmer driving a cow came along and quietened the horse.

'I'll — I'll not ride again,' said Hans. 'There's a devil inside that beast. Just look at its eyes! How wild they are! Not like the gentle eyes of that cow of yours.'

'Do you fancy the cow?' said the farmer, knowing very well that the horse was worth three times as much as the cow.

'I do indeed,' said Hans.

'Then she's yours,' said the farmer, and he put the cow's halter into Hans' hand.

'What a lucky fellow I am,' Hans thought, as the farmer mounted the horse and rode off at a trot. 'Here I am with a big fat cow all to myself. Whenever I'm thirsty she'll give me milk; and once home, my mother will not lack for butter or cheese.'

Busy with his thoughts, Hans walked along with his cow at a slow pace for the sun was still hot and there was little shade.

Presently, he came to a village and tether-

ing his cow to the nearest post, he went into the village inn and spent his last halfpenny on a small glass of cider.

Refreshed and still feeling amazed at his luck, Hans set out again. Now, he had to cross a lonely moor and pretty soon he was just as thirsty as before and longing for a drink.

'What a fool I am,' thought Hans suddenly. 'I can milk my fine fat cow. There's nothing more refreshing than a drink of milk.'

Once again, he tied up his cow. Then he took off his cap. 'It's not as good as a pail,' he said to himself, as he crouched down by the cow. 'But she won't know the difference.'

Alas, the cow deeply resented Hans' clumsy efforts to milk her. And, finally, with a loud protesting moo, she kicked out and knocked Hans to the ground with a good deal of force.

Scarcely knowing what had hit him, Hans lay there, seeing stars, until a butcher, who was taking a short cut across the moor, came upon him and pulled him to his feet.

In fact, the butcher was taking one of his pigs to market in a wheelbarrow, and he told Hans this as soon as Hans was ready for conversation. 'It's a fine young porker,' said the butcher, 'and I'll be sorry to part with it.'

'So it is!' said Hans, giving his cow a very reproachful look. 'So it is!'

'You weren't thinking you'd get any milk out of that old cow,' went on the butcher, 'She's far too old for milking. But there, that's your business. You'll get some beef when you send her to the slaughter-house.'

'I don't care for beef,' said Hans. 'Never have liked it, nor does my mother. On the other hand, she loves pork. So do I.'

'Then we'll make an exchange,' said the

butcher with a greedy glint in his eye, which Hans failed to notice. 'Your cow for my pig!'

'Done!' cried Hans. 'What a lucky fellow I am! But are you quite sure?'

'Don't worry about me,' said the butcher, with a jovial laugh. 'I like to give folks a helping hand whenever I can.'

And with that, the butcher put a rope round the pig's neck and lifted it out of the wheelbarrow. 'There you are,' he said. 'All yours!'

As Hans set out once again, he smiled and whistled to himself, so happy was he.

'It's unbelievable, my luck!' he said aloud. 'Here I am with a fine pig of my own and with the prospect of goodness knows how many fine dinners.' And he licked his lips at the vision of sizzling pork and string upon string of fat pork sausages.

With a light step and a singing heart, Hans crossed the moor and was just about to take the road to the second village, which he had to pass through, when he met a boy carrying a goose.

The boy threw the pig a knowing glance before saying, 'That's a fine pig you have there.'

'And that's a very fine goose,' said Hans.

'It should be,' said the boy. 'It's meant for a christening and we've been fattening it up for eight weeks or more.'

Hans was about to go on his way when the young lad suddenly cried out, 'Hi, there! It's just occurred to me. That pig you've got there — it looks exactly like the one that was stolen from our village yesterday.'

Hans turned back with a look of alarm on his face. 'You don't say!' he exclaimed.

'I do say!' said the boy. 'And if I were you I'd keep away from that village. The Mayor himself is looking for that stolen pig. He'll almost certainly clap you in chains and put you in a dark cell if he catches you.'

At this, Hans began to look more and more alarmed. 'What on earth can I do?' he asked.

'My legs are beginning to shake at the very thought of these chains you mention.'

'I tell you what,' said the boy, 'I'll take your pig. It's not much of a bargain for the goose is as fat as butter but I'm after helping you and I won't be going near the village for a bit.'

Quick as a flash Hans handed over the pig and tucked the goose under his arm, whereupon the lad made off at a run, laughing to himself, as he went.

'My, what a lucky fellow I am,' Hans said to himself, as he walked into the village. 'We'll have roast goose for dinner and the fat will give us dripping to spread on our bread for supper. And when I think of it, these goose feathers will give me the softest pillow in the kingdom.'

Smiling to himself, Hans took a firmer hold on the goose and looked about him. His merry eyes lighting on a scissors-grinder, and being full of high spirits, he stopped to greet him.

'It's a grand day,' said Hans cheerfully. 'I see you're busy.'

'Of course I'm busy,' said the grinder, eyeing the fat goose. 'There are always plenty of folk who need their scissors sharpened. That's why I can put my hand in my pocket and always find gold.'

'That's more than you can say about me,' said Hans, still smiling. 'I haven't a half-penny to bless my name, but I do have this very fine goose, so I'm not complaining.'

'Where did you buy it?' asked the grinder.

'I didn't buy it,' said Hans. 'I exchanged it for my pig.'

'And the pig?' asked the grinder. 'Where did you get that?'

'Oh,' said Hans, with a loud laugh. 'I got it in exchange for my cow.'

'And the cow?' asked the grinder, and he stopped work altogether in his interest.

'Why, I exchanged my horse for that!'

'And the horse?'

'Oh that! Why I gave a lump of gold as big as a turnip for the horse.'

'And the gold?' queried the grinder.

'Why that was my wages for seven long years of service,' said Hans.

'Well done!' exclaimed the grinder. 'I do congratulate you. You're a clever fellow, I see, and not easily made to look a fool.'

'I've been in luck all the way,' said Hans.

'And now there's not many miles to go before I hand over the goose to my mother.'

The grinder took another long, careful look at the goose. Then he said, 'If you were me — you would never need to worry about making your fortune. Didn't I tell you my pockets were always filled with gold?'

'You did,' said Hans. 'What's your secret?'

'There's no secret,' said the grinder. 'All you have to be is a grinder like me. I tell you what, I'll give you this grinding stone — it's a trifle worn but no matter — in exchange for your goose. What do you say?'

'You're a generous fellow,' cried Hans in delight. 'And I'm a lucky one to be sure.'

And he handed over his goose to the grinder and accepted in exchange a grinding stone.

'I like you,' said the grinder, as he tucked the goose under his arm. 'I tell you what — I'll throw in another stone for good luck. You can use it to hammer out nails.'

Hans accepted this second stone, which truth to tell, was just an ordinary stone, with a merry smile, saying, 'Now, I'd best be on my way. There's not much farther to go.'

As he set out on the last few miles for home Hans couldn't help telling himself again what a lucky fellow he was.

Then he came to the last field which separated him from his mother's cottage, 'I'll stop here,' he decided, 'and have a drink from the well.'

With the greatest possible care, Hans lifted the heavy stones on to the stone wall and sat down himself a moment. How his arms ached, and his feet too. It had been no joke carrying the two heavy stones for such a distance.

But after a moment's rest, he felt better and bent over to take a drink from the well. As he did so, his arm knocked against the stones, and they slipped into the well, hitting the water with a loud splash.

Far from feeling sad at his loss, Hans suddenly threw his cap in the air. Then he began to jump for joy.

'Was there ever a man so lucky!' he shouted to the birds. 'Without these two heavy stones, I can run all the rest of the way home to my mother!'

And with a heart as light as thistle-down, he sped across the field.

Rumpelstiltskin

There was once a miller whose only daughter was more beautiful than words can properly describe. The miller was poor and had little to boast about but his daughter.

Now, one day, he found himself in the King's presence and in order to keep his end up the foolish miller began boasting about his only daughter.

'Not only is she beautiful,' he said, 'but she can spin straw into gold.'

'Indeed,' said the King, and for the first time he looked at the miller with interest. 'Then she must come to the palace and prove herself. I will provide her with the straw and she will give me the gold.'

The miller trembled with fear when he heard this but he dared not refuse, for the King was known to have a very hot temper.

The next morning he presented his daughter to the King who took her to a small room in the palace tower.

'Here is your spinning wheel and your reel,' he said. 'And there is the straw which the old miller says you can spin into gold. If you fail to do this you will lose your head.'

And then he left her, locking the door behind him.

The poor girl sat looking at the straw, despair in her beautiful eyes. She couldn't spin straw into gold; nobody could! So in the morning the King would come, take her away and cut off her head.

At such a dreadful thought, hot tears ran down her pale cheeks and she began to sob.

All at once the door opened and through it pranced a little man, no higher than her waist and dressed in green.

'What will you give me if I spin that straw into gold for you?' asked the manikin without even bothering to explain who he was.

'This gold ring on my little finger,' replied the girl.

The little man nodded as if satisfied and sat himself down at the spinning wheel. By morning all the straw was spun into gleaming gold.

After his royal breakfast, the King climbed up to the turret room not knowing what to expect. When he saw the heap of gold, he was speechless with delight.

'You have done well,' he told the girl, 'but I would like to test you yet again.'

And he had the girl taken into a larger room which could hold more straw.

'Now,' said he, 'spin all this straw into gold by morning. If you fail to do so you will lose your head.' And off he went.

The poor girl felt more desperate than ever as she stared at the heap of straw until all at once the door opened and in came the tiny man.

'What will you give me if I spin that straw into gold for you?' asked the manikin.

And the miller's daughter replied, 'You can have my necklace with four pearls in it.'

The little man took the necklace, sat down at the spinning wheel and began to spin. By morning all the straw was spun into gleaming gold, and the girl smiled happily.

She was still smiling when the King came to her room. And he, too, smiled in delight at the sight of so much gold.

But the mound of glittering gold made him long for still more. So once again he said to

the girl, 'You have done well, but I would like to give you one more test. If you pass, then I will make you my wife and you shall be Queen of all the land.'

And he led the miller's daughter into a room which was twice as big as the last and filled almost to the ceiling with straw.

'Now,' said the King, 'spin all this straw into gold by morning. If you fail, you will lose your head. If you succeed, you will be my Queen.' And then he left her, locking the door behind him.

Immediately he was gone, the girl burst into loud sobs until all at once the door flew open and in came the manikin.

'What will you give me if I spin that straw into gold for you?' he asked.

'I'm afraid I have nothing left,' the girl answered sadly. 'Nothing at all!'

'Then promise to give me your first child if you are made Queen,' said the manikin.

And the miller's daughter thought, 'Why, it might never happen. That's the kind of promise I can easily make.' So she made it.

Then the little man sat down at the wheel and by morning all the straw was spun into gleaming gold.

When the King came to the room and found it filled with gold, his pleasure knew no bounds for now he was the richest King in the whole world.

'You have done well,' he said, 'I will marry you tomorrow and you shall be Queen of the land.'

So the poor miller's daughter became a King's wife and very quickly grew accustomed to her new life, and forgot all about her promise to the little man.

A year passed and to the King's delight she presented him with a beautiful baby girl.

Even then she did not spare the manikin a single thought until one day the door of her royal chamber suddenly opened and the little man stood before her.

'I have come to claim the child,' said the manikin. 'Remember your promise!'

Horrified, the Queen began to weep and so desperately did she sob that the little man had pity on her. 'I will take no treasure from you,' he said, 'I want only the child. But if you can find out my name within the next three days, I will release you from your promise. You can keep the child and you will never see me again.'

All that day and all through the night the Queen tried to guess his name. Could it be James or William or Henry or Oscar? Perhaps it was a name like Caspar or Jonah?

But when the little man came on the first day and the Queen told him all the names she had thought up, the tiny man said, 'That is not my name . . .'

On the second day, the Queen sent her own servants far and wide to find out uncommon names — names like Sheepshanks and Crookback and Lacelegs.

But when the little man came and the Queen repeated these names and many others, all he said was, 'That is not my name.'

On the third day, the Queen sent one of her servants into the next kingdom, saying that he must not return until he could bring her a list of new names.

'Alas,' said the servant that night, 'I have not been able to find a single name that is new.'

At these words, the poor Queen began to weep. 'Then all is lost,' she whispered, and she broke into loud sobs.

'There is only one thing, Your Majesty,' said the royal messenger, 'that struck me as being very odd.'

The Queen raised her head, 'Whatever it was,' she said, 'tell me.'

'Having crossed the valleys and followed the course of rivers,' replied the servant, 'I turned my attention to the hills and steep mountains . . .

'It was on top of one of these that I came upon a sight so strange that I cannot forget it. There, hopping and prancing round a fire was the smallest man I have ever seen. And, what's more, as I watched, this little man started to sing . . .'

'Yes, yes, go on,' urged the Queen, her eyes suddenly alight. 'What were the words?'

'Strange words,' answered her servant. 'They went something like this:

'Today I bake, tomorrow I brew.

Soon the Queen's child will be here.

How glad I am that no one knew

That I am Rumpelstiltskin dear.' '

At this, the young Queen clapped her hands in delight. 'That's it!' she exclaimed. 'That is his name!'

Soon afterwards, the little man himself appeared, and the Queen began saying, 'I know your name — it's Harry and if not Harry, then it must be Crispin.'

'That is not my name,' answered the dwarf.

'Then it is Rumpelstiltskin,' said the Queen quietly.

'The devil has told you!' screamed the tiny man in a rage and, purple in the face, he ran from the room and was never seen again by the lovely young Queen.

Little Brother, Little Sister

There was once a little brother and a little sister. Everyone called them Little Brother and Little Sister because they were never seen apart. So that's what we shall call them.

One day, Little Brother said to Little Sister, 'Since our dear mother died and our father married again, we have never known a single moment's happiness.'

'Our new stepmother gives everything to that ugly daughter of hers,' said Little Sister. 'I try to love her because she has only one eye, but she is so rude and greedy that I can't.'

'I can't either,' said Little Brother, 'and what's more, I can't bear to watch her have so much to eat when we get only crusts.'

'Let's run away,' said Little Sister.

'We'll go very early in the morning,' said Little Brother.'

The next morning, Little Brother and Little Sister ran away. They crossed broad meadows and fields and walked by the edge of woods until they reached a deep dark forest.

'It's growing late,' said Little Sister, 'and I'm very tired.'

'Let's find a hollow tree and make it our bed,' said Little Brother at last.

So, hand in hand, they went into the dark forest, and when they found the right kind of tree, they lay down and fell fast asleep.

When next they opened their eyes, it was morning.

'Come,' said Little Brother, 'we must make our way through this forest.'

But, as they walked, the sun came out and soon Little Brother vowed he was dying of thirst.

'We'll soon find a brook and there you can have a drink,' said Little Sister.

Now, I should tell you, if you haven't already guessed, their cruel stepmother was really a witch and, being a witch, it was easy for her to follow the children and listen to what they were saying. Straight away, she laid a terrible spell on all the burbling brooks in the forest.

When the children came upon their first brook, Little Brother bent down eagerly and was just about to drink, when all at once his sister heard the words, 'If you drink me you will turn into a tiger, tiger, tiger.'

'Stop!' cried Little Sister. 'The water is bewitched, I'm sure of it. Do not drink or you will turn into a tiger and eat me.'

This, by the way, is exactly what the witch *hoped* would happen.

So Little Brother did not drink. 'Very well,' he said, 'I'll wait until we come to the next spring.'

But when they came to the next spring, and Little Brother bent down to drink, his sister heard the words, 'If you drink me you will turn into a wolf, wolf, wolf!'

'Stop!' cried Little Sister. 'The water is bewitched, I'm sure of it. Do not drink or you will turn into a wolf and tear me to pieces.'

So Little Brother did not drink.

But when they came to the next brook, Little Brother was so thirsty that he bent down quickly and drank before his sister had time to cry out.

Instantly, he took the shape of a young roebuck!

'Little Brother, oh poor, dear brother!' sobbed his sister. 'What will become of us?'

The little roe wept, too, as he lay down beside her. Then Little Sister dried her tears and taking off her golden garter she put it round the roebuck's neck. Then she made a rope out of long rushes and fixed this to the collar.

'Come,' she said, trying to smile through her tears. 'We will look for a place where we can stay together for I will never leave you, dear brother.'

Little Sister led the roe farther and farther into the forest, and the roe followed obediently after her.

Night was beginning to fall when at last Little Sister came to a clearing in the forest, in the middle of which, was a small hut.

With the roe at her heels she ran towards it hoping that it was empty. The hut was bare inside but it felt snug and warm after the forest, and Little Sister clapped her hands in delight as she looked about her.

'From now on this will be our home!' she cried.

Soon Little Sister had found enough moss and leaves to make a soft bed for her brother. The little roe lay down on the soft, mossy bed and Little Sister lay down beside him with her head on his body and in this way they fell fast asleep.

In the morning, Little Sister went out into the forest where she found big, juicy berries for the roebuck's breakfast so that he need not go out.

But Little Sister could not keep the roe inside the hut for ever or tether him to herself as they went out for walks in the forest.

With each passing day, the roe grew bigger and stronger and, with each passing day, he grew more and more restless.

'Little Sister,' he would say at night-time when they were ready to sleep, 'tomorrow let me go free. I long to run in the forest and feel the wind in my face.'

'Not yet,' Little Sister would reply. 'Not yet, dear brother. Be patient. One day you will be so big and strong that no other wild creature will be able to harm you. Then I will set you free, but not before!'

This seemed to satisfy the roebuck who loved Little Sister with all his heart, but he could not hide the restless look in his soft brown eyes whenever the wind whistled through the trees.

Then one day something happened which made Little Sister more fearful than ever for her brother.

Huntsmen came to the forest and from far away she could hear their shouts and the baying of their hounds.

The strong, young roebuck pricked up his ears and began to move restlessly about the hut and Little Sister watched him anxiously.

'I cannot stay here quietly when I hear the hunters' horns,' he said to his sister at last. 'Set me free, Little Sister! Set me free!'

But Little Sister flung her arms around the roe and begged him with all her heart not to go out into the forest that day.

Early the next morning, however, the hunters came again to the forest and this time their leader was the King himself, a handsome young man with a golden crown set firmly on his head.

Once again Little Sister heard the sound of the horns and the baying of the hounds, and the roebuck heard them too.

'I cannot stay here quietly when I hear the hunters' horns,' he said to his sister. 'Set me free, Little Sister! Set me free.'

And once again Little Sister flung her arms about the roe and begged him with all her heart not to go into the forest that day.

But this time the roebuck would not be quietened, and Little Sister had to let him go. She opened the hut door and away he bounded, beautiful in the sunshine.

That day the huntsmen were more than ever eager to show off in front of their young King. And so, when they caught sight of the beautiful young roebuck among the trees they sounded their horns and gave chase.

But no matter how hard they galloped they could not draw near enough to harm the roe with their guns.

And that night the roebuck returned home to Little Sister, his eyes shining with the excitement of the chase.

Early the next morning, the King and his huntsmen came once more to hunt in the green forest.

Once again, the young roebuck heard the sound of their horns and the baying of their dogs. 'Set me free, Little Sister! Set me free,' he began to plead.

And Little Sister, knowing that nothing she could say would change his mind, went to the door and opened it wide.

Away bounded the roebuck, beautiful in the sunshine as he sped through the trees.

This time the King and his huntsmen drew near enough to the roebuck to wound him in the leg. But, as before, the roebuck seemed to gather speed when it reached a certain part of the forest and then simply vanished from sight.

'You must not hunt tomorrow,' Little Sister told her brother when she saw his wound.

'Bathe it for me; it is nothing,' her brother replied. 'But if the huntsmen do not come to the forest I will stay at home.'

Little Sister wept when she heard this for she was certain that the huntsmen would come looking for the roebuck.

And she was right! Once again the sound of the horns rang through the forest and once again the roebuck made for the door.

'Wear your golden collar today,' Little Sister begged. 'Perhaps it will protect you from harm.' And she fastened the collar round the roe's neck before he bounded away.

That day the King and his huntsmen chased the roe the length and breadth of the forest but they did not try to shoot at him.

As nightfall came, the roebuck wearily made for home and the King followed him at a safe distance.

From his hiding place in the bushes, the King saw the roebuck run through the open door of a hut in a clearing of the forest. And he caught a fleeting glimpse of a lovely young girl.

The King waited until the stars were out

then he went to the door and knocked. It was opened by the same lovely girl he had caught sight of some hours before.

Never in all his life had the King gazed upon any one so beautiful and the girl, as she looked into the King's merry eyes, felt her heart beat faster.

'I care not who you are,' said the King, taking off his golden crown. 'All I know is that I desire to make you my wife. Come back to the palace with me.'

'I will only consent to be your wife,' the young girl replied, 'if my roebuck comes with me to your palace.'

'The roebuck will never leave your side,' replied the King. 'He will be safe and always protected from harm under my care.'

So Little Sister and the roebuck left the hut in the forest and went to live in the King's great palace. And Little Sister married the handsome King and was happy the whole long day with nothing else to wish for except that her dear brother be restored to her in his true shape.

Now, one day, news reached the wicked stepmother that Little Brother and Little Sister still lived.

'I meant them to be dead by now!' she said to her ugly, one-eyed daughter. 'The thought that the girl is now Queen fills my heart with black envy. I will bide my time and use my magic powers when I can see a way to destroy her.'

A whole year passed and then a beautiful baby boy was born to the young Queen. When the wicked witch heard this, she disguised herself as an old country woman and went to the palace to ask for the job of chamber-maid. This was given to her. So now she was close to the Queen she hated.

Soon she saw a way to destroy her.

Early one morning the King left the Queen all alone and went out hunting. The old witch, who had by now invited her daughter to come and stay at the palace, saw her chance and took it.

'Your bath is ready, your Majesty,' she called out to the Queen. And as soon as the Queen was inside the bathroom the witch filled the room with steam and the Queen sank to the floor, overcome with heat.

The evil stepmother waited until night fall. When it was dark she placed her own daughter in the King's bed and gave her a resemblance to the Queen though she could not give her two eyes.

That night the King returned in high spirits and the old woman called out, 'The Queen rests in bed; do not draw the curtains but let her sleep in peace.'

Now the stepmother had it in her heart to take the new-born baby and destroy it, but that night the true Queen came to life and visited the baby in his cradle. Nor did she forget to find the roe and talk to him gently until the first streaks of dawn appeared in the sky.

'Her Majesty walked the palace at midnight whilst you slept in your own chamber,' one of the guards told the King.

The King was astonished for he thought his Queen had slept the whole night through in her curtained bed.

'I will keep watch tonight,' he vowed, 'and if my Queen walks in her sleep I will take her in my arms and wake her.' The King waited in his hiding place until the tall, graceful form of the Queen appeared. Then he grasped her in his arms and in that very moment the Queen was restored to full life again.

Quickly she told the King all that had happened to her, and the King called out to his guards to arrest the evil chamber-maid and her daughter.

Judgement was soon passed upon them and they were condemned to death by burning, for it was the law of the land that all witches must burn at the stake.

As the witch burnt, her evil spell over the roebuck was broken and he took his human shape again. As for the one-eyed daughter — she escaped and fled into the forest where she was eaten by a bear.

So now, the gentle Queen and her loving husband had nothing to fear, and they lived together in great happiness.

Little Brother made the palace his home and in time he married the King's sister.

Clever Elsie

There was once a pretty young woman called Elsie. She did so many silly things that the people in her village nick-named her Clever Elsie in a spirit of fun.

Now Clever Elsie lived with her mother and father who took care of her as best as they could but longed to see her safely married.

'Who will have her?' Elsie's mother would ask herself. 'All the young men in town know how silly she is!'

Then, one day, a handsome young stranger came to the town. His name was Eric and quite by chance he very soon met Elsie and liked her.

He made up his mind quickly that he would like to marry her and he went off to see her father. 'I'll marry her tomorrow,' he told Elsie's father, 'providing she will make me a clever wife for I cannot abide silly women.'

That night, as they sat round the supper table, Clever Elsie smiled prettily at her new fiancée, and her mother and father looked at her with approval.

Presently, Elsie's father said, 'Elsie, my girl, take this jug and go down to the cellar to draw some beer.'

'Certainly, I will,' said Elsie, who was most anxious to make a good impression on Eric. 'I won't be long.' And off she went.

Now I should tell you that the cellar held a number of large barrels all filled with beer and all Elsie had to do was to turn the tap and let the beer run out of one of these barrels.

'Eric will be delighted when he sees how fast and well I can perform tasks,' Elsie told herself, as she ran down the stone steps which led into the cellar.

When Elsie reached the cellar she put her jug under one of the beer barrels, turned on the tap and then began looking about her.

To her horrified amazement she saw, just above her head, and resting on the barrel itself, a big, wicked-looking pickaxe which had been left behind by one of the masons who had been working in the cellar.

Clever Elsie stared at the pickaxe and then cried aloud, 'Woe is me! When I marry Eric we're sure to have a child and when he is big enough we're sure to ask him to come down

99

here to draw beer. Then that pickaxe will fall on his head and kill him.'

And with that thought uppermost in her mind, she forgot all about the beer and burst into loud sobbing.

Meantime, upstairs, her mother and father and Eric sat patiently waiting for Elsie.

At last her mother asked their serving woman to go down to the cellar and find out what had happened to their daughter.

The maid found Elsie sitting beside the barrel of beer and crying her eyes out.

'Whatever is the matter?' she asked. 'The master and mistress are growing impatient.'

'Alas,' sobbed Elsie, 'If I marry Eric, we're sure to have a son and when he is big enough,

we're sure to ask him to go down to the cellar and draw beer. Then that pickaxe will fall on his head and kill him.'

To this, the maid replied, 'Lord love us! What a Clever Elsie you are!' And she sat down beside Elsie and began to cry.

Ten minutes passed and down into the cellar came the old serving man. When he saw Elsie and the maid weeping together, he said, 'Tell me now, what's the trouble, for the mistress sent me to find out?'

And Elsie sobbed, 'Alas, if I marry Eric, we're sure to have a son and when he is big enough we're sure to ask him to go down to the cellar and draw beer. Then that pickaxe will fall on his head and kill him.'

To this, the old serving man replied, 'Lord love us! What a Clever Elsie you are!' And he sat down on the other side of Elsie and began to wail in distress.

Presently, Elsie's mother came down to the cellar and when she asked what was wrong, Elsie told her, 'Our future son is going to be killed by that pickaxe up there, for when he's big enough we're sure to ask him to go down to the cellar to draw beer for us.'

Then Elsie's mother threw up her hands in horror at the thought and exclaimed, 'Lord love us! What a Clever Elsie you are!' And sat down behind Elsie to join in the weeping and wailing.

Time passed. Upstairs, Elsie's father was now red in the face with impatience and, at last, he too went down to the cellar.

But no sooner had Elsie sobbed out her story than the father exclaimed, 'Lord love us! What a Clever Elsie you are!' And sat down beside his wife. Soon he too was snivelling into a large handkerchief.

When Eric found himself all alone he began to think that something very odd must be going on in the cellar. And presently he got up and went to see for himself.

Imagine his surprise when he found the whole family and the two servants sitting in front of the beer barrel and in tears!

'What is it?' he asked. 'What has happened to make you all so sad?'

'Alas, dear Eric,' sobbed Elsie, 'our future son is going to be killed by that pickaxe which is balanced on top of the beer barrel. So you see we have good reason to be sad.'

'I see what you mean,' said Eric. 'What a Clever Elsie you are to think so far ahead. My mind is made up. I'll marry you tomorrow.'

So Elsie and Eric were married and for a time they were very happy. Then one day Eric told his wife, 'Our money is now all finished. I must go out in search of work and you must go into the fields and cut the corn so that we can have some bread.'

'Very well, dear Eric, I will go at once,' said Elsie.

As soon as Eric had gone to search for work, Elsie went into the kitchen and made herself a bowl of delicious soup.

'I will take this into the field with me,' she told herself.

But when Elsie reached the field her legs were weary with walking and she made up her mind to eat first before cutting the corn.

After she had finished up the bowl of soup, she began to think she should go on resting for a while.

So she lay down among the tall corn and fell fast asleep.

The whole afternoon passed. Eric came home and was surprised to find that Elsie had not yet returned with the corn. 'What a Clever Elsie she is!' he thought to himself. 'She works on and on even though it grows dark.'

But as the night wore on Eric began to think that he had better go out to the fields and help his wife carry the corn home.

He soon found Elsie, still fast asleep, and not one single bit of corn cut. Suddenly the scales fell from Eric's eyes. 'Clever Elsie indeed!' he exclaimed. Then he ran home and fetched a net with bells on it — the kind of net he used to scare away birds. When he returned to the field he draped this about the sleeping Elsie and stole away.

When it was quite dark Elsie woke up. The bells made such a jingling and jangling as she ran homewards that the little sense she had left her completely.

'Who am I?' she asked herself as she came to her house. 'I never made this noise before. Can it really be me?'

When she tried the door she found it locked and barred and this made her feel more than ever doubtful. 'This can't be my house,' she told herself. 'The door is always open.'

Then she went to the window and called out, 'Eric, dear Eric, is Clever Elsie inside?'

'Certainly she is,' replied Eric, coming to the window.

'Alas then, this can't be me!' wailed Clever Elsie. And, taking to her heels, she ran down the street and out of the town and, do you know, she was never seen again!

102

The Old Woman of the Mountains

A long, long time ago when the world was quite young, there lived an old woman on the side of a tall mountain.

Summer and winter this old woman, who was very old indeed and walked with the aid of a crutch, would hobble down the mountain until she came to the forest that surrounded the mountain on three sides.

Once there, she would collect grass for her flock of geese, which she loved like her own children, and then fill her two baskets with all the wild fruit she could find.

Now, if by chance a villager stumbled on her as she worked, he would look the other way and hurry on. For it was said in the village that the old woman was a witch.

One day, at the height of summer, the old woman left her little house on the mountainside and went, as usual, to the forest, and her geese, as usual, watched her go.

When the old woman reached the clearing in the forest she began to gather grass for her geese. Then she filled her two big baskets with wild apples and pears.

As she worked, a tall, fine-looking young man came wandering through the forest. His keen eyes took in the great load of grass and the baskets already heavy with fruit.

'Good-day, old woman,' he said, addressing the witch. 'You work hard for your years. Have you a son who will come and carry your burden for you?'

'I have no son,' said the old woman, as she straightened her back. 'My only support is that crutch you see lying there.'

'Who will carry this load?' asked the young man. 'It is too heavy for you.'

'You have young legs,' replied the old witch. 'You're young and strong and perhaps accustomed to hard work?'

'I'm young, it's true,' laughed the youth, 'but hard work has never come my way for I'm a rich man's son — a Count in my own right!'

The old woman gave him a long, hard stare. Then she said, 'Nevertheless you have kind eyes. Would you see your own mother carry such a weight?'

'Certainly not!' cried the Count.

'Then you will help me with my bundles,' said the witch. And before the young man could say a word, she hoisted the load of grass on to his back and hung the baskets of wild fruit on to his arms.

Seeing that he was trapped into helping her, the Count laughed. 'Very well, little mother,' he exclaimed, 'I will carry your bundles for you!'

So the Count and the old woman set off and the sun beat down on them as they made their way through the forest.

Presently, the Count's footsteps began to

falter and he cried, 'Old woman, this load is almost too much for me. I am weary and faint already.'

The old woman, who had been hopping along behind with the aid of her crutch, drew level with him. 'What! Tired already!' she cackled. 'And you so tall and straight and strong!'

'I may be all these things,' panted the Count, 'but the day is hot and I am not used to carrying such heavy loads.'

'It is not so much farther,' comforted the witch. 'Keep going, good sir! You will get your reward when you arrive.'

The young man tried to put down the baskets but somehow or other they would not budge from his arms. And with the witch's cackling laugh in his ears, he took a few more plodding steps forward.

As for the old woman, she seemed to grow younger and more active with each step, and presently, without a word of warning, she took a flying leap and landed on top of the heap of grass.

In vain, the Count tried to shake her off. In vain, he protested that he could hardly take one more step, so weary were his legs. The old witch took no heed, but kept urging him on.

Almost too tired to answer the jibes of the old woman who taunted and teased him in turns, the young man at last reached the mountain and began the long hard climb upwards.

'Faster! Faster,' urged the old witch, from her perch. 'It is not far now.'

'I can scarcely keep on my feet,' moaned the young man. 'Would that you and I had never met!'

And for the hundredth time he tried to lay down the baskets and shake the old woman off his back. But in both these tasks he failed for the baskets stuck to his arms and the woman stayed firmly on her perch.

The poor Count was so worn out that he was ready to drop. 'I cannot take another step,' he gasped. 'Have mercy, old woman!'

'There is little farther to go now,' she replied with another shrill cackle, 'and if you will raise that handsome head of yours, you will see that I speak the truth.'

With a mighty effort of will, the exhausted Count raised his bowed head and saw almost in front of him a little house, scarcely more than a hut, only a few yards away.

At the sight of the old woman, the flock of geese stretched their long necks and began to honk loudly in greeting. Their mistress then skipped nimbly down from the Count's back.

'Lay down your load,' she bade him, and she smiled up into his face. 'I am grateful to you for your effort and you will have your present after you have rested.'

Wearily, the young man put down the baskets of wild fruit and his load of grass, and the geese honked all the louder and flapped their wings as he did so.

As they stood outside the hut, a tall woman, strong in appearance but hideously ugly, came towards them with a question already forming on her pale lips, 'What kept you so late, mother dear?' she asked, with down-cast eyes.

And the witch told her, 'Nothing — nothing at all, daughter, except that this young man who kindly helped me with my load, found the way so hard that he walked slowly.'

Then, as the woman still stood there, the

witch went on sharply. 'Come, we'll go into the house together for I have no mind to leave you all alone with him.'

'There is no need to worry on that score,' the young man protested, hiding a smile, for it sounded as if the witch thought he might try to make love to the poor, ugly creature. 'I will rest under this apple tree until my strength returns.'

'Do that,' said the witch, 'and afterwards I will give you your present.'

The Count stretched himself out on a bench beneath the tree and was soon fast asleep.

Who knows how long he would have slept had not the witch roused him at dusk.

'You cannot stay longer,' she said. 'Go now, but take this gift and look after it well.'

Then the witch handed him a little box cut out of a single emerald. The Count, feeling completely restored again, thanked her warmly for already he had forgotten all that he had suffered on her behalf, and set off down the mountainside. When he reached the bottom, he did not know which direction to take and for three days and three nights he wan-

dered aimlessly in the forest, completely lost.

On the fourth day, he found a path which, instead of taking him in circles, led directly out of the forest. And after an hour's steady walking he found himself approaching a strange town.

No sooner had he entered this strange town than he was met by soldiers and taken before the King and Queen.

The Count, surprised and somewhat afraid, began hurriedly to give some explanation for arriving with neither baggage nor servants.

Then, on a sudden impulse, he brought out the witch's small emerald box and offered it to the Queen, knowing that inside it was a single pearl of rare beauty.

As soon as the Queen set eyes on the pearl she fainted away and the King, thinking the box was enchanted, had his soldiers drag the poor Count off to prison.

But that same night, as the Count lay in his dark cell, the Queen sent for him.

Finding himself once more in the presence of the Queen, the Count bowed low, not daring to speak.

'Young man,' said the Queen in a voice that trembled with emotion, 'I have sent for you in order to tell you a story. At the end of it you will understand why you must tell me everything you know of the emerald box and the pearl it contains.'

The Count would have spoken, but the Queen silenced him with a majestic wave of her hand.

'Three years ago,' she went on, 'my husband, the King, thought much about his end and, wishing to be assured of our daughters' love, he sent for them.

' 'How well do you love me?' he asked of our eldest daughter. And she replied, 'I love you, dear father, as I love the sweetest sugar.'

'Then my husband turned to our second daughter and asked her the same question, and she said, 'I love you, dear father, as I love my prettiest dress.'

'The turn of our youngest daughter came next,' continued the Queen, catching her breath in a sob, 'And she, above all, the King loved for she was not only good and gentle but had a rare beauty. Her golden hair shone like sunbeams and her cheeks were as pink and white as apple blossom.

' 'How well do you love me?' my husband asked our youngest daughter. And she replied, after a long moment's silence. 'I have found, dear father, that we cannot do without salt to taste our food. So, father, I love you better than I love salt.' '

The young Count had listened with absorbed attention to the Queen's words. Now, he cried, 'How wise your youngest was to say such a thing!'

The Queen sighed. 'Alas, my husband heard her words in deep anger. He considered that she had insulted him by comparing her love to salt, and turning to our other daughters, he cried out, 'Your youngest sister is not worthy of the love I have borne her all these years and she shall have no share in my kingdom.' Then he divided up all his treasures between them and, beside himself with grief and rage, banished our youngest from the land. We have not set eyes on her since that day,' finished the Queen, burying her face in her hands to hide her tear-filled eyes.

'All that you tell me is strange and sad,' said the Count at last, 'but I do not understand, Your Majesty, what part my emerald box plays in your story.'

The Queen looked up and said slowly, 'Your box, young man, contained a pearl, did it not?'

'That is true,' answered the count, 'a pearl of unusual beauty.'

'My daughter,' said the Queen softly, 'wept pearls instead of tears. No one knows how she came to have this gift. All we know is that if she shed tears, pearls fell from her eyes. When I saw the pearl in your emerald box I knew it was a tear from my youngest daughter's eyes.'

'Then she must be somewhere!' cried the count. 'We must search for her and restore her to you.'

'Her father has long ago repented,' answered the Queen, 'and lives only in the hope that he will see her again, but we have searched in vain.'

'That old woman on the mountainside beyond the forest might know something of this matter,' the count said. 'It was she who gave me the box.'

Then he told the Queen his story. And when he had finished, the Queen said, 'We

shall set out for this mountain without delay and we shall go without carriages or servants. You will be our guide.'

The young Count waited impatiently while the Queen informed her husband of their plan and the King, overcome with joy at the thought of perhaps finding his long lost daughter, quickly arranged to be absent from the palace.

Meantime, far away on the mountain beyond the forest, the old witch sat at her spinning wheel. She worked quietly and busily until the loud honking of the geese told her that her daughter had returned from the well.

'Come, daughter,' she called out, 'it is time for your spinning,' and the tall, strong woman who was so hideously ugly, entered the room and sat down at a second spinning wheel.

They worked on in silence until dusk fell. Then the old witch spoke once again.

'It is time for you to go down the mountain and into the forest,' said the old woman.

And her daughter rose obediently.

'Go to the stream where the three oaks grow,' went on the witch. And her daughter nodded.

The moon came up in the dark night sky as the young woman ran lightly down the mountainside. When she reached the stream by the three great oaks, she peeled off the skin which covered her head and all the top part of her body. And this she hung up on a tree to dry after washing it in the running water of the stream.

Then she sat down by the stream and in the soft light of the moon she was more beautiful than words can tell. Her hair shone like sunbeams and her cheeks were pink and white like delicate apple blossom.

The girl sat there, without moving, until somewhere beyond the three great oaks, a twig snapped.

She looked up, then, in sudden alarm, fear filling her beautiful eyes. She was like a wild animal poised in sudden flight.

For some moments a deep silence hung over the forest until once again came the sound of a twig snapping. And this time the girl really did take fright.

Snatching the skin from the branch where it was drying she turned and fled away through the trees, running as swiftly and as lightly as a roe. But before she began her climb up the mountain she stopped and pulled the skin over her face and shoulders.

When she arrived at the hut, she flung open the door and gasped out her fears to the old witch who still sat at her spinning wheel.

'I heard a noise in the forest,' she panted. 'I was afraid that human eyes had seen me as I really am. I ran like a roe deer back to you, dear mother, but oh, how my heart beats!'

'There is nothing to be afraid of now,' said the old witch. 'Help me to make the hut clean and tidy for soon we shall have visitors.'

Then rising from her seat, the old woman put a brush into her daughter's trembling hands and encouraged her to begin sweeping.

When the house shone like a new pin and not a speck of dust was to be seen, the old woman beckoned her daughter to her side.

111

'Listen well, little one,' she said in a voice that was low and gentle, 'for I declare the time has come for you to leave me.'

At this, the girl cried out, 'No, no, no little mother! You have cared for me and I have given you my heart and my love. Where could I go? What would become of me?'

The old woman stroked the ugly skin that hid the beauty of the girl's own cheeks.

'I, too, will leave this place,' said she. 'It has served its purpose and you have not been unhappy here these last three years.'

'But for you I would have died or perished in the forest,' said the girl. 'And this miserable skin has protected me from those who would have taken advantage of my beauty. Besides, as you know, my life has always been in danger . . .'

'Perhaps, perhaps,' said the witch, 'but no longer . . . Now, this is what I wish you to do. Go into your room. Take off the skin and put on the silken gown which you were wearing when I found you in the forest.'

Now, perhaps you have guessed already that the snapping of the twig which had so alarmed the witch's daughter was caused by no less a person than the Count himself. And this is how it came about.

The Count had led the King and Queen far into the forest and then lost the way which was not surprising, for the forest was riddled with a maze of paths all of them leading nowhere.

The royal couple, unaccustomed to exercise, were almost too tired to go on and the Count, taking pity on their weary legs, suggested he try to find the way to the mountain by himself. 'Then I will return for you,' he had said. And the King had readily agreed.

Thankful that the moon had risen and there was light enough to see, the Count began his search and, after an hour or more, suddenly spied among the trees the witch's daughter.

'Now, I have only to follow her,' he told himself joyfully, 'and she will no doubt lead me to her mother.'

To his surprise, the woman was making for a small stream and, when he saw her stop, the young man hid himself behind one of three big oak trees close by.

Imagine his further surprise, when suddenly the woman peeled off the skin of her face, shoulders and arms and, after washing it, hung it on a branch to dry.

Now, he found himself gazing upon a maiden of such beauty that his heart missed a beat. Her hair shone like sunbeams and her cheeks were pink and white like apple blossom.

The Count scarcely dared to breathe as he peered at the girl from his hiding place, but he moved carelessly. A twig snapped once and then, minutes later, another twig snapped. He saw the girl lift her head in sudden alarm. Then, before he could make his presence known, she had snatched the hideous skin-mask from the tree and fled.

The young man had made a gallant attempt to follow, but the kindly moon which had served him so well as a lantern, was suddenly hidden by a dark cloud, and he soon lost sight of his beautiful quarry.

Nevertheless, he was now going in the right direction and, to his joy, he came upon the King and Queen.

'When we felt rested,' the Queen told him, 'we continued our journey on our own account.'

The three travellers went forward until, at last, they reached the foot of a tall mountain, which the Count instantly recognised. 'Above is the old woman's hut,' he cried. 'And, look, there is a light in her window!'

With joyful steps, the royal couple made their way up the mountainside and when they reached the hut, the Queen crept to the window and looked inside. 'I can see nothing but an old dame at her spinning wheel,' she said. 'But, oh, how neat and tidy the room is. Not a speck of dust to be seen!'

As she spoke, the Count knocked at the door,

and the old woman called out, 'Come inside. I have been expecting you!'

Then, as they stood looking down upon her, she went on, 'You could have spared yourself much heart-ache if you had only acted in love and justice.'

'We have learned our lesson,' replied the Queen, with a sob. 'Our only wish is to see our beloved daughter once again.'

'And so you shall,' said the old woman, 'for when I found her in the forest I brought her here and have kept her from all harm.'

Then she crossed the room and called softly, 'Daughter, little daughter, you may come out now. I am ready for you.'

The door opened and the Princess came into the room, clad in a shimmering silken gown.

She was so beautiful that the Count loved her from that moment though he said never a word but only gazed at her.

As soon as the Princess saw her mother and father standing there, speechless with joy, she ran to them and kissed them and hugged them as if she would never let them go.

Then, as the Queen began to shed tears of happiness, the Princess turned to the Count. a faint blush staining her soft cheeks.

The two looked deep into each other's eyes and the Count's eyes told her how much, how very much, he loved her.

'How foolish and unjust I have been!' the King exclaimed at last. 'Having divided all my treasures between your two sisters I have nothing left for you, my dearest child.'

'She needs nothing,' said the old woman. 'When she wept over you, I saved the pearls that fell from her eyes, and I have kept them safely these past three years. They are worth all the rarest treasures of your kingdom put together — and more.'

And when the princess ran to her, her arms outstretched, the old woman, who certainly could *never* have been a witch, cried, 'And I give you, besides, this little house!'

And so saying she vanished from their sight.

There was the smallest rumble as if the old mountain itself was saying goodbye and the little house trembled slightly. But when the King and Queen looked about them they found it had become a splendid palace!

Without wasting any time, the Princess and and Count were married. They made their home in the palace on the mountain where they lived very happily for ever afterwards.

The Four Clever Brothers

Once upon a time, when there was much more fun in the world than there is today, a man said to his four sons, 'I am poor and so have nothing to give you. You are now of an age to go into the world and learn a trade.'

Then the man told his sons to return to him in four years' time so that he could judge how well they had fared.

The four brothers left the house together, but when they came to crossroads, the eldest said, 'Here, we should separate. Each of us will take a different road, but we will do as our father says and return in four years.'

It was not long before the eldest son met a man who asked him where he was going.

'I'm going to learn a trade,' the boy told him, and the stranger replied, 'I'd be glad to teach you a trade. Come with me and learn how to be a thief.'

Now the eldest son had no wish to end his days on the gallows and he said as much, but the thief promised to make him so smart that nothing would be safe from his hands. And at last the eldest agreed, thinking that he need not use this skill to become a thief.

The second brother also met a man.

'Where are you going and what do you hope to do?' the stranger asked him, and the second boy replied, 'I am going to learn a trade.'

'Then come with me and be an astronomer,' said the man. 'If you become an astronomer you will see everything through a telescope. Nothing will be able to escape you.'

The second brother thought it would be a fine and noble thing to be an astronomer and he said as much. So it was agreed, and at the end of his four years' apprenticeship his master gave him a telescope of his own.

'Nothing can ever be hidden from you if you use your telescope,' the astronomer told him, before the young man set out for home.

Meanwhile the third brother had come upon a skilled huntsman who promised to take him into his service and teach him his craft.

At the end of his four years' apprenticeship his master gave him a gun, saying, 'Accept the gun as a token of my esteem. It will never let you down. You will always hit the object which you aim at.'

As for the youngest brother, rather against his will, he learned how to be a tailor. 'It's not a very exciting trade,' he said to his new master on the first day.

'In that you are mistaken,' said the tailor, 'for I am going to teach you how to sew anything you desire. It could be as soft as cheese or as hard as steel. No matter — you will be able to sew it with tiny, invisible stitches.'

At the end of four years' apprenticeship, the skilled tailor gave his pupil a needle which would sew anything together no matter if it was as soft as cheese or as hard as steel.

The four brothers met at the crossroads as they had promised each other they would.

'Let us return quickly to our father,' said the eldest, after they had exchanged news.

Their father received them joyfully, and they told him what they had learned.

'I would like to test your skills,' said their father, and he took them outside.

As they sat down beneath a large tree, the father looked upwards into its branches and said, 'High up among the branches is a nest

five eggs from beneath the chaffinch without as much as disturbing one of her fine feathers.

'Well done,' said the father. 'Now, it is your turn,' and he looked at the huntsman who was leaning on his gun. 'You shall show me how well you can shoot.' And he placed the five eggs in cups and stood them on a bench.

'Nothing easier,' boasted the huntsman, guessing his task.

'Ah, but you must shoot them in the middle and with a single shot,' his father told him.

The huntsman, with a smile, raised his gun and took aim. With one shot he hit all five eggs.

'Excellent!' praised his father. 'Now we must see if my youngest son can do equally well by stitching up these five eggs.'

'That's simple,' said the clever tailor, and taking out his needle he began sewing the eggs together, and not a single one of his stitches was visible to the naked eye.

'You are everything that you said you were!' exclaimed the delighted father, as he stood up. 'I am proud of you, though I cannot yet say which of you is the most clever.'

The four brothers remained contentedly at home after that, each one practising his art to the best of his ability.

The brothers were good friends and by sharing their skills they managed to make enough money to keep both themselves and their old father in reasonable comfort.

with a chaffinch sitting on her eggs. Tell me how many eggs are in the nest.'

The astronomer looked through his telescope. Then he said, 'I can see five eggs.'

'Now,' said the old man, turning to his eldest son. 'You say that you are a clever thief. Prove it then by fetching down the eggs on which the chaffinch sits — without disturbing the bird in any way.'

'It shall be done,' said the clever thief, and he began to climb up the tree. When he reached the topmost branches, he stole the

How long this state of affairs would have continued no one really knows, but something happened which changed everything.

The King lost his only daughter, a gentle and beautiful girl, to a dragon. A blight fell on the whole country, then. There was no laughing or singing or dancing, and the old King himself went into mourning.

Finally, his counsellors advised him to issue a proclamation saying, 'If any man is brave enough to rescue my daughter from the dragon who carried her off, that man shall be her husband.'

It was not long before the brothers heard about this proclamation and they decided to do something about it.

'At least I can tell you her whereabouts,' said the astronomer, and he brought out his telescope and looked through it. 'I can see the Princess sitting on a rock in the sea,' he went on, 'and the dragon is guarding her.'

'Let's tell the King,' said the youngest brother.

'We'll ask him for a ship,' said the third brother.

The King gladly gave the four brothers a ship and they sailed away across the seas.

The astronomer guided their ship in the direction of the rock where the Princess sat with the dragon's tail round her waist and his head on her lap.

'The dragon's asleep,' said the astronomer. 'You could shoot him easily.'

But the huntsman shook his head. 'It's not

As the dragon slept on, the brothers made for the open sea, laughing and shouting at each other in their excitement.

But their excitement soon changed to fear when the tailor chanced to look upwards.

'The dragon is after us!' he cried.

Belching a cloud of black smoke, which was really his breath, the dragon circled the ship, before attacking. He delayed a second too long, for it gave the huntsman time to snatch his gun and shoot the monster through the heart.

The dragon fell like a thunderbolt on the ship, and so big and heavy was he that the ship began to break up under his weight.

Two of the brothers ran to the Princess and put her between them as they jumped into the sea.

Soon they were joined by the tailor and the thief. The tailor began proving his skill by sewing two planks together which served as a boat so that for the moment they could consider themselves safe from the waves.

'I fear our ship is lost,' said the thief.

'Not so,' answered the tailor, 'for if you help me to gather the pieces, I can sew them together again.'

Confident in the power of their brother's wonderful needle, the others did what he asked, and the tailor repaired the ship with a speed that was truly remarkable.

In no time at all the ship was afloat and sailing for home.

The four brothers then delivered the young Princess into her father's arms and the King wept tears of joy at the sight of his long lost daughter.

'One of you shall have her as your wife,' said the King at last, 'but which one?'

The brothers stood aside and began then to argue fiercely among themselves.

'If it hadn't been for me . . .' began the astronomer. But he was shouted down by the thief, the tailor and the huntsman.

At last, they turned to the King for his opinion. 'It seems to me,' said the King,

as simple as it looks,' he said. 'My bullet might harm the Princess.'

'Then I will try my skill,' said the thief. 'I will land on the far side of the rock and steal her away.'

The thief was as good as his word and so quietly did he move that he had the King's daughter safely on board ship without waking up the dragon.

'that all four of you equally deserve the hand of my daughter. Since this is not possible, I will give to each of you half a kingdom instead.'

The brothers were delighted when they heard this and gladly accepted, for truth to tell none of them *wanted* to get married . . not even to a Princess!

The Six Fortune Hunters

There was once a young soldier called Hans. At the end of the war, however, Hans found himself with only a few pence and no job. This made him angry for he had given the best years of his life in fighting for his King.

'If only I could get on in the world,' he told himself, 'I would then be in a position to put my case before the King. He would surely listen to me if I were more important.'

And with that thought in his mind he began walking through a deep forest. As he walked he saw a man plucking up trees.

'Why,' thought the young ex-soldier, 'that man has the strength of a regiment. He up-roots trees as if they were plants.'

Then he went up to the strong man, who was as bald as a coot, and said, 'Will you be my servant? Together we shall make our fortune.'

'I will,' said the strong man, 'but first I must take this bundle of firewood home.' And he picked up the trees and tucked them under his arm.

They had only gone a little way when they came upon a hunter.

'What are you shooting at?' Hans asked him. 'For you are aiming your gun at *something!*'

'About two miles distance a fly is sitting on a tree trunk and I intend shooting off one of its legs,' the huntsman told him.

'Good gracious me!' Hans exclaimed. 'If you can shoot that well you must join us. We three will certainly get on in the world.'

'I will,' said the huntsman.

All three walked along until they left the forest and began to cross a broad meadow.

There, they came upon seven windmills with their sails whirling round as if blown by a mighty gale.

'Now, that's a strange sight,' said Hans, 'for there's not a breath of wind anywhere, not enough even to stir the grass.'

They walked on for another two miles or so until they came upon a merry little man, in red cap and red stockings to match, who was seated on a tree trunk. He was holding one nostril and blowing out of the other.

'What are you doing?' Hans demanded.

'Nothing much,' answered the little man, 'I'm just blowing the sails of some windmills in the big meadow.'

'Good gracious me!' exclaimed Hans. 'If you can blow that well you must join us. We four will certainly get on in the world.'

'I will,' said the blower, and he got up and began walking along beside them.

After a while they saw a young man who had taken off one of his legs and laid it beside him. Hans stopped in his tracks.

'What a strange sight!' he exclaimed, and he stared at the man who was standing on one leg, a pleasant smile on his handsome face.

'Not really!' said the young man. 'You see I am a runner and I have to take off one of my legs to stop myself from running too fast. If I run using both legs I can run faster than a bird can fly.'

'Good gracious me!' exclaimed Hans. 'If you can run that well you must join us. We five will certainly get on in the world.'

'I will,' said the runner, and he picked

up his leg and set off beside Hans and his companions.

It was not long before they met a young man, gaily dressed in blue and orange but with his cap completely covering one eye.

When Hans saw the foolish way in which the stranger wore his cap, he said, 'You look a real fool with your cap over one eye, if you will forgive me for saying so. Why don't you straighten it?'

'I dare not,' replied the man, 'for if I do, frost will cover the earth and all the birds and soft little creatures will then be frozen to death.'

'Good gracious me!' exclaimed Hans. 'If you can make such a terrible frost then you must join us. We six will certainly get on in the world.'

'I will,' said the man.

Presently the six friends came to a strange town where notices were pasted to every wall.

'*Whoever runs the race with the Princess and wins, will be her husband,*' said the notice. And then in small print, it said, '*but whoever loses the race with my daughter, loses his head.*'

Hans read the notice twice. Then he looked at the runner. 'You can win this race for me and I, being your master, will then marry the King's daughter.'

Now the King's daughter was the fastest runner in the whole kingdom and no one expected the young servant to win the race for his master.

Great crowds turned out to watch as the two runners were handed empty pitchers.

'You must fill your pitcher at a well six miles away from here and race back with it,' the King told the young runners.

Then a pistol was fired and the runners started off.

Soon the young man had disappeared from sight. He ran so fast that he had reached the well and filled his pitcher with water before even the young Princess was half way there.

On the way back the runner felt sleepy and, knowing he had hours to spare before the Princess could possibly catch up with him, he made up his mind to have a short rest. He looked around for a place where he could lie down and chose a soft bed of leaves under a nearby tree.

Then he spied the skull of a long dead donkey which had been left there to rot and taking this he used it as a pillow.

'I'll just have forty winks,' the young runner told himself as he unstrapped his leg.

Then, with his pitcher full of water beside him, he lay down, put his head on the donkey's skull and was soon fast asleep.

Meantime, the young Princess had made good progress. She ran swiftly, as swift as any deer, and not a single drop of water did she spill from her pitcher.

When she came upon the sleeping runner she smiled in high glee.

'I'll teach him to think he can outrun me,' she said to herself. And with that, she bent down, picked up the runner's pitcher and emptied its contents on the grass.

Then she sped on, certain now that she would win the race, for even if the runner awoke he could not hope to win the race if his pitcher was empty.

But the runner slept on and who knows

how long he would have slept if Hans, being anxious to know what was happening, had not asked the huntsman to spy out the land for him and report all that was taking place.

'I have already seen too much,' said the huntsman, 'for with my sharp eyes I have seen the Princess play a very mean trick on our sleeping runner.' And he told Hans what the Princess had done.

'You say our runner still sleeps,' said Hans. 'Then the race is already lost.'

'Not so,' said the huntsman, and he raised his gun. 'I will shoot the pillow from under the sleeper's head and so waken him.'

The huntsman did this and the runner awoke instantly. When he saw that his pitcher was empty, he strapped on his second leg and as swift or swifter than any bird could fly ran back to the well.

Now he had much time to make up if he were going to win the race but the runner showed no sign of fear.

On and on he raced, back to the well, and then with a full pitcher he turned himself about.

And so fast was his time that he reached the winning post ten whole minutes before the Princess who had tried to win by a trick.

Now the King and the Princess were very angry at the result of the race. 'I do not wish to marry such a very common young man,' declared the Princess bitterly.

'And neither you shall,' said the King, 'for I have thought of a way out.' And he asked the six friends to go with him to a room where they would feast and be merry. This room had a floor of iron and doors of iron and the window was barred with iron bars.

The King stood at the door and showed them a table inside the room which was heaped with good things to eat. But when the six were inside the room the King bolted the iron door. Then he sent for his chef and told him to make a big fire under the floor of the room. For he meant the six companions to die from suffocation.

As the six companions ate their way through the big feast, they were suddenly conscious of being unpleasantly hot.

'The King means us to perish in this room,' said Hans. 'I can see it all now. There must be a huge furnace under this iron floor.'

'We shall die of suffocation!' cried the huntsman.

'It's a fine end to our fortune hunting,' said the runner, beginning to choke.

'I have always dreaded fire,' murmured the strong man. 'There is so much of me to roast!'

'There must be a way out for us,' cried Hans, desperately eyeing the bolted door and the narrow, barred window, 'but I am afraid we are trapped.'

'Not so,' said the little man with the cap over one eye. 'You have all forgotten what I told you about myself. Did I not say that I can make a frost that will freeze to death all the creatures of the world?'

'Indeed you did!' gasped Hans, who was now very hot and finding it difficult to catch his breath.

'Then watch!' said the little man, and he put his cap straight on his head.

Immediately there came such a frost in the room that the food on the table froze to the plates, and the wine in the big goblets was frozen solid like lumps of red rock.

All six friends could breathe freely once again, and they began to laugh.

Meantime, the King was now certain that his six troublesome companions were being slowly suffocated to death.

'Never fear, daughter,' he said to the Princess, 'you will not be obliged to marry that common soldier. No man has ever before left my iron room — that is to say, alive!'

But, to his anger and dismay, when the King went at last to see the result of his evil plot, he found the six fortune hunters not only alive but making merry.

'The flames could not have been fierce enough,' he told himself, and straightway he

stormed down to the bakehouse to find his unfortunate chef.

'You shall perish in your own miserable fire,' snarled the angry King, when he came face to face with his fat, good-natured cook.

And the poor man could do nothing but point to the hot flames that were rising upwards.

'I tell you, sire, these six men must be wizards if they have escaped my heat,' said the cook at last. 'You had best get rid of them for no ordinary man could survive my lovely big fires.'

The King began to think that his cook was right and so he sent for the six friends.

'I tell you what,' he said, addressing himself to Hans. 'If you will leave my kingdom I will give you as much gold as one of your servants can carry.'

'I agree,' said Hans. 'Give me as much gold as my servant can carry and your pretty daughter will be left to choose her own husband. I will send for the gold in fourteen days' time.'

Then Hans went away and summoned all the tailors he could find. 'Make me a sack!' he ordered them. 'It must be the biggest sack the world has ever seen.'

When the sack was made the only person who could lift it was the strong man, the man who could uproot trees as if they were plants.

'Take it to the King,' Hans told him.

'What does that giant fellow want with me? Why does he carry a bundle the size of a house on his back?' demanded the King, when he saw him.

'I have come for the gold,' said the strong man. 'It is to go into this sack.'

Then the King emptied his treasure house of gold, and all of it went into the sack.

'It is not enough,' said the strong man.

At that, the King sent out for more gold and it came in barrows and carts and still the sack was only three-quarters full when the strong man tied it up and lifted it on to his broad back.

Then before the astonished eyes of the King,

he strolled away with it — out of the palace and through the town — until he came to the forest where his friends were waiting for him.

'Now we shall live like lords for the rest of our lives!' Hans cried. 'Our fortunes are well and truly made.'

Hans and his friends were half way out of the kingdom, before the angry King made up his mind to send a regiment of soldiers after them and take them prisoners.

The galloping soldiers had no difficulty, however, in catching up with the six friends.

'Halt!' screamed the brave young captain. 'Put down that sack of gold and stay where you are or we shall cut you to pieces.'

'You don't say!' said the blower, and quietly he put one finger to his nostril and closed it. Then he blew through the other nostril and, lo, the soldiers were all at once tossed into the air like tiny shreds of paper on a windy day.

'And that's that!' laughed Hans. 'Come, gentlemen, let us continue on our way.'

When the King heard what had happened to his regiment, he cried, 'Let these six fortune hunters go! I know now my cook was right. They *are* magicians and we are well rid of them!'

The Three Spinners

There was once upon a time a poor widow woman who had a very lazy daughter.

Time and again she would tell the girl to get on with her spinning so as to earn some money and, time and again, she found the girl sitting by the window, dreaming.

One day, the mother lost her temper and began to beat the girl about the shoulders for her laziness.

Now, it just so happened that the Queen was passing by in her carriage and could not help but hear the screams coming from the widow's house. 'Stop the carriage!' she ordered.

Then the Queen, who was by nature extremely curious, went up to the house to enquire what the screaming was all about.

The poor widow woman was greatly upset at the sight of the Queen on her doorstep and even more upset at the idea of telling her that she was the mother of a lazy girl.

So when the Queen asked her about the screams, she answered, 'Well, it's like this, Your Majesty, my daghter wants to spin all day long and half way through the night as well, but I am too poor to give her the flax.'

'Is that why you were beating her?' the Queen asked in surprise.

'It was,' said the woman. 'I wanted her to leave off spinning and it was the only way to make her do so.'

The Queen thought a moment, then she said, 'There's nothing I like better to hear than the sound of a spinning wheel. Give me your daughter. I will take good care of her at the palace and see that she has all the flax she needs for her spinning.'

The widow woman was greatly pleased at this. 'You must go with Her Majesty,' she said to her daughter. 'From now on you will be living at the palace.'

But when the Queen took the girl back to the palace she left her in a room that was heaped high with flax.

'Now spin this flax,' commanded the Queen,

'and when your task is completed, you shall marry my eldest son as a reward.'

'How can any one as lazy and unskilled as I am, hope to spin all that flax?' the widow's daughter asked herself in dismay, when she found herself alone. 'What will happen to me when the Queen finds I cannot spin . . .?'

And she went over to the window and stared out, her heart as heavy as lead. Presently, she saw coming towards the window three tall women and she noticed something strange about each one. The first had a huge foot, broad and flat. The second had an enormous underlip that stuck out a mile from her chin; and the third had a great broad thumb which looked very clumsy and horrid.

When the three women saw the glum face of the girl at the window, they asked her what was wrong.

'Everything!' confessed the girl. 'And in another minute I shall burst into tears. Here I am shut up in a room that's filled with flax and there's the Queen thinking that I can spin the lot.'

On hearing this, the three strange women consulted together, then one of them said, 'If you will invite us to your wedding, whenever it may be, and not be ashamed to call us aunts and make a fuss of us in public, we will help you to spin the flax.'

'Oh, I will do that most certainly,' cried the girl, beginning to smile. 'Come to the door and I will let you in.'

And she rushed to the door and opened it. Then she showed the three spinners — for that is what they were — the great heap of flax.

'Leave it to us,' they said. The first spinner sat down at the spinning wheel and with her big, broad foot trod the wheel. The second spinner with the ugly underlip sucked the thread, and the third spinner used her enormous thumb to twist the thread, and each time that she struck the table with her thumb a skein of yarn fell to the floor.

The women worked all night and in the morning the flax was spun into yard upon yard of the finest yarn.

'Now, don't forget your promise,' they said to the widow's daughter as they prepared to leave. 'We shall expect to hear from you.'

'I won't,' said the girl, 'and thank you very much.'

Not long after the women had departed, the Queen came to see how the spinning was going. She was so delighted at the sight of all the finely spun yarn that she gave orders for the royal wedding to take place at once.

'I have three aunts,' said the girl. 'They must come to my wedding for they have been so good to me.'

'By all means,' said the Queen graciously.

'I want them to sit at my table,' went on the girl, 'so that I can make a fuss of them.'

'Of course,' said the Queen.

The Queen's son was a handsome young man, and quite delighted to have such a wonderful spinner for a wife, and the girl was equally pleased and flattered to become a Princess overnight.

So the wedding was a very joyous affair and the three spinners were well received and invited to sit near the bride and bridegroom.

As the new Princess made them welcome, her husband asked, 'Forgive me, but how did you come by that broad flat foot?'

And the first spinner to whom he had put the question, answered, 'By treading; by treading!'

Then the Prince asked the second spinner if she would tell him how she came by her underlip that stuck out so, and she answered, 'By sucking; by sucking!'

And the third spinner added quickly, 'And I got my ugly thumb by twisting the thread.'

'They are all wonderfull spinners, you see,' said the Princess, feeling embarrassed.

'And all wonderfully ugly,' whispered the King's son. 'You shall never touch a spinning wheel again, my beloved, for I could not bear you to become like them.'

So things turned out well for the widow's daughter — perhaps much better than she deserved!

The King of the Golden Mountain

Long ago, there was once a rich merchant who was blessed with two children, a little boy and a little girl.

The children were still tiny when their father negotiated a business deal, sending out two of his ships laden with all his treasures. If the two ships crossed the seas safely, then the merchant stood to gain great wealth.

Alas, a storm blew up when the ships were far out to sea and both were sunk, their loss leaving the merchant a poor man.

When he heard the dreadful news, the merchant left the house and set out on a long walk. His steps led him into an empty field where, with a sad face and bowed head, he paced up and down.

Lost in his miserable thoughts, the poor merchant did not see the small black dwarf at his side until he spoke.

'What ails you?' asked the little man.

'I would tell you if I thought you could be of any comfort,' said the merchant.

'Perhaps I can,' retorted the dwarf.

So then the merchant told his sad story, and the dwarf said at the end of it, 'It is clear that you set great store on being a rich man. You shall be twice as rich as before if you will promise to give me the first thing that greets you on your return home.'

Then, as the merchant hesitated, the dwarf added, 'I will come back for it in twelve years' time.'

'It's most likely to be my dog,' thought the merchant to himself. 'And twelve years is a long time.'

'What do you say?' pressed the little man. And the merchant nodded. 'I agree.'

Then the dwarf made him write down what he had promised on a piece of paper and sign it.

But when the merchant reached home, it

was not his dog that greeted him first, but his little boy, who had managed to crawl to the door unobserved.

With a shock of dismay the merchant remembered his promise to the dwarf.

'Was it only a joke?' he asked himself, and he began to wish that it was. But some time later when he had a reason to go up to the attic to search for some old papers, he found on the floor a great heap of money.

Then the merchant knew the dwarf had been true to his word, and he was afraid.

As the years passed and his son reached the age of twelve, the merchant grew more and more sad. When his son questioned him, the merchant told him about the black dwarf and his promise which could not be broken.

'Do not be sad,' said the boy bravely. 'Let us go to the field together, but first I will ask the priest to bless me.'

When this was done, father and son set out for the field, and the son made a circle round himself and his father.

Shortly after this was done, the manikin was at their side though he could not enter the circle. 'You cheated my father into a promise he should never have made,' said the boy in a loud clear voice.

'That is not so,' said the black dwarf. 'You belong to me now. My race is the enemy of all mankind and you are one of us.'

But the manikin had not the power to compel the boy to accompany him, so he said, 'You do not belong to your father, that is certain. Seat yourself in that boat on the river and let it take you where it will.'

Watched by his anxious father, the boy went to the river at the bottom of the field and climbed into the small boat that was moored to a stake.

'Now, push the boat out,' the dwarf ordered the father, and the merchant did so.

To his horror, the merchant saw the boat turn over in the water and, thinking that his son must surely be drowned, he went home and mourned for him.

But the boy was not drowned. Instead, he drifted away downstream with the boat — until at last he found himself on a strange shore which he set out to explore.

After a short while he came upon a great castle and thinking that there he would find rest and shelter for the night, he entered.

Now, although he did not know it, the castle was enchanted and the boy, after going from one empty room to another, came at last to a room where a snake lay coiled in a ring.

To his surprise, the snake spoke to him. 'Do not turn away from me,' the snake said. 'This castle and the whole kingdom is in the power of the black dwarfs. You, alone, can save my father's kingdom and restore me to my proper self.'

'What must I do?' asked the boy.

And the snake, who was really a Princess, told him 'Tonight and for two nights follow-ing, twelve black dwarfs will visit me. When they see you, they will ask you who you are but you must not answer them, or utter a single word. They will beat you and torture you and on the last night cut off your head, but do not utter a single groan. If you can endure all that they do to you, you will break the spell and I will restore you to life again.'

'I agree,' said the boy, 'for I would like to overcome these wicked dwarfs.'

Everything happened as the Princess had said it would. And on the third night the twelve black men cut off the boy's head.

But that night, the snake changed back into a beautiful Princess, and she restored the boy to life again.

Indeed, the whole castle came to sudden life. Doors opened and shut, servants fled up and down the long corridors; dogs began to bark; and horses stamped and neighed in the courtyards.

The lovely young Princess threw her arms about the boy who was no boy at all in her eyes, but a brave hero, and proposed that they should get married immediately.

'This is the land of the Golden Mountain,' she told him, 'and you shall be its King.'

So, amidst great rejoicing, the two were married and began a happy life together.

As the years passed, the Queen gave birth to a fine baby boy and the King, now that he was a father himself, thought of his own father and longed to see him again.

When he told the Queen that he had a mind to journey to the land of his father, she wept and begged him not to go. But the King of the Golden Mountain had made up his mind and nothing would make him change it.

'Then take this ring,' said the Queen. 'It is a wishing-ring. When you put it on your finger your wish will be granted. Promise me, however, that you will never wish for me to leave this palace and be by your side.'

'I promise,' said the King, and he put the ring on his finger and wished that he was outside his father's town.

Now, the King of the Golden Mountain had been so long away from his true home that he had forgotten how the people looked and how they dressed.

He did not think that his own appearance was strange, until the sentries at the gate of the town barred his way.

'Who are you? And what country do you come from?' demanded the sentries. 'Your attire is so strange we must know your business before we can allow you to enter our town.'

'I am King of the Golden Mountain,' the King told them.

But at this the sentries laughed in a mocking way, never having heard of such a place, and turned him away.

Then the King went into the hills where he found a shepherd who was willing to exchange his poor rags for the richly coloured costume that he was wearing.

When next the King presented himself at the town's gates, the sentries took him for a shepherd and let him pass.

The King made his way to his father's house, certain that his father would know him at once. But this was not so for the merchant had, long ago, given up his son for dead.

'It is true,' said the merchant, 'I had a son, but alas he was drowned. If this is some trick to obtain food and shelter then you are welcome to come inside and eat.'

'It is true that I am dressed in the garb of a humble shepherd,' replied the young man. 'But I asure you that I come from a country where I am known as King of the Golden Mountain. I swear I am your son and I have my birthmark to prove it.'

Then the King rolled up his sleeve and showed his father the mark on his right arm, and the father recognised it.

'You are indeed my son,' he cried joyfully. 'But do not spoil my joy with lies about being a king.'

'I am not only a king,' came the reply, 'but a husband and a father. My wife and son live with me in a palace, splendid beyond words.'

When the father began to laugh at this, the King of the Golden Mountain, in a sudden rage, twisted the wishing-ring on his finger. 'I wish for my Queen and my son to be at my side,' he muttered.

They appeared instantly and the merchant was convinced at last of the truth of his son's statement. But the Queen wept and told her husband that he had broken his promise and that only evil would be the outcome.

The King would not listen. Instead he took her and his son to the stream where the black dwarf had put him in the boat, and then they sat down by the bank.

Presently, the King fell fast asleep, and the Queen, with a glint in her eye, took the wishing-ring from his finger and wished herself and her son back in her own kingdom.

When the King awoke, he found himself all alone and the wishing-ring gone.

'I cannot return to my father's house,' he thought to himself, 'for if I do he will take me for a magician and want nothing more to do with me. So I must find a way to get back to my own kingdom.'

For some time, he wandered the country until he came upon three giants. They were enormous men and seemed about to do battle with each other.

'What's the trouble?' the King asked.

And one of the giants told him, 'Our father, who was the most powerful giant in the land, has died and left us our inheritance.'

'But we do not know how to share it out,' said another of the giants. 'Little men have big brains, they say. Perhaps you can help us.'

137

'What is your inheritance?' enquired the King. 'Tell me and I will decide for you.'

'A sword which will cut off anyone's head at the word of command,' the smallest of the giants told him. 'And a cloak which renders its wearer invisible, and a pair of high boots that will carry their wearer to any place he so desires.'

'I must try these things out to prove their worth before I give judgement,' said the King.

And he took the cloak, put it on and vanished from their sight. When he appeared again, he asked for the sword.

'You have only to hold the sword and say the words, 'Let all heads roll', the shortest of the giants told him. 'That's all!'

'Give me the sword,' said the King, 'and I'll give you my word that I shall try it out on that tree over there.'

So the giants gave the King their magic sword, and the King cut the broad trunk of the tree in two as if it had been butter.

Certain now that the King was an honest fellow, the giants willingly handed over the boots.

'I'll try them for size,' joked the young man. 'Perhaps they will be too big for me.'

'They'll fit you all right,' said the middle giant, bending over to peer more closely at the King. 'They're magic boots and will shrink to size.'

With the invisible cloak over one arm and the sword in his hand, the King then slipped his feet into the magic boots.

For a moment he hesitated. He did not want to cheat the giants out of their inheritance for they had done him no harm. On the other hand, the boots would take him into his own kingdom. The longing to see his lovely wife and his little boy was so strong in him that he began to wish to be with them.

Instantly, he found himself transported into his own kingdom. As he drew near to his palace, the King was greatly surprised by the sound of merry music and singing.

Soldiers and servants were running this way and that and they were smiling as if they were just about to take part in a festival.

'What is it? What is all the bustle and the music about?' asked the King, taking a firm hold of one of the servants.

The man did not recognise his former lord and master for the King was still dressed as a lowly shepherd.

'It's none of your concern, I am sure,' the servant said impertinently, 'but if you must know, our Queen is marrying again today and has invited us to join in the celebrations.'

At this, the King's brow creased in anger, and his eyes grew dark. He turned away from the servant, who ran on, leaving him alone.

Then the King pulled his magic cloak about him so that he was invisible to all eyes and entered the palace.

He made his way to the great banqueting hall where his lovely Queen sat at the head of a long table piled high with exotic foods. Knowing that he was invisible, the King took up a position behind his wife's chair.

As she laughed and talked to the man at her side, the servants waited upon her. But no sooner did she raise a goblet to her lips than it was taken out of her hand by the

invisible King. Her plate, too, was quickly emptied — though not a morsel of food passed her lips.

Frightened and guilty, the Queen at last got up and fled from the table.

The King followed her to her room and when they were alone, he shed his invisible cloak.

'Miserable woman!' the angry King shouted. 'You have wasted no time in finding yourself another to take my place.'

The Queen wept and begged for mercy but the King, in his terrible rage, pushed her roughly to the ground. Then, leaving her there, he returned to the banqueting hall.

'The feasting is at an end,' he shouted in a voice of thunder. 'Return to your homes, for I am your true King and there can be no other as long as I live.'

'What mad fellow is this?' the guests began asking each other. 'A wild-looking shepherd with a sword in his hand!'

Then they began to laugh and tease the tall figure before them until the King spoke once more.

'I tell you,' he said, 'I am your true King and if you will not accept me — then may the gods protect you from your blindness.'

He waited, but not a single voice was raised to proclaim him king.

'Very well,' said the King. 'Let all heads roll except mine!' And all heads did roll!

In this strange manner did he overcome his enemies and ruled once more as King of the Golden Mountain.